PRIMAVERA'S ODYSSEY OF DISCOVERY

had taken her to a town where destruction, poverty, ignorance, and prejudice held sway. It was a place so ugly that even her magical voice could not sing it back to beauty. But worse than this burned-out city were the giants who fed its impoverished masses—creatures who made their living through slaughter, and would not hesitate to take advantage of her if they ever learned her secret.

Then she found Elysia, and with her very first song, Primavera was hailed with the same ardor that had greeted her own family when they set the city rocking a generation earlier. Yet her parents had discovered not only the brightness of Elysia but its dark reflection known as Under, where the Old Ones went to wait for death.

And when Primavera, too, went Under to help the one friend she'd found in Elysia, she risked forever losing the magic which gave her whole world light. . . .

PRIMAVERA

Francesca Lia Block

A Roc Book

ROC

Published by the Penguin Group
Penguin Books USA Inc., 375 Hudson Street,
New York, New York 10014, U.S.A.
Penguin Books Ltd, 27 Wrights Lane,
London W8 5TZ, England
Penguin Books Australia Ltd, Ringwood,
Victoria, Australia
Penguin Books Canada Ltd, 10 Alcorn Avenue,
Toronto, Ontario, Canada M4V 3B2
Penguin Books (N.Z.) Ltd, 182–190 Wairau Road,
Auckland 10, New Zealand

Penguin Books Ltd, Registered Offices:
Harmondsworth, Middlesex, England

First published by Roc, an imprint of Dutton Signet, a division of
Penguin Books USA Inc.

First Printing, June, 1994
10 9 8 7 6 5 4 3 2 1

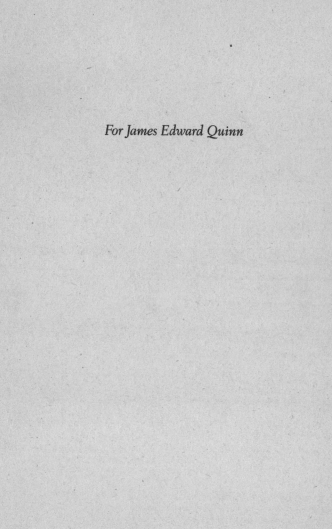

For James Edward Quinn

PROLOGUE

Somewhere deep in the desert was a lush garden
that had sprung up suddenly when a group of
people arrived and played a song of resurrection,
changing everything. The lands, scaly as a lizard's
skin, became moist, the once-gray rocks shim-
mered green as if submerged in water. There
were orchards where fruits swelled with sweetness on the branches, dropped into waiting
hands; streams, so clear and bright they could be
mistaken for sunlight, ran between the rows of
trees; purple, green, blue, white, and crimson
butterflies covered the trees like petals, then
suddenly exploded back into sky. A band of wild
horses had found this place; from somewhere
over the dunes they came running. Flocks of
birds, too, came from some unknown distance
and their feathers fell sometimes in the gardens

like plumed flowers bright on the paths. The flowers themselves grew rootless in the branches of the trees or grew from the earth taller than the tallest man; sitting in their shade was a balm to all sorrows, as was bathing in the tumbling, clear, fish-sparkled, water-lily-bridged body of water that was named the Sound.

This place, the people said, is all because of the five who came here—the child, the mother and the father, the gardener and the mage. Ecstasia, they called themselves.

The child was like a small garden herself—her hair falling to her waist and always full of petals, her skin glowing with a pollen dust of sun, her body dancing on air, it seemed, like the tree flowers, her feet wet from wading, leaving a path of new blossoms as she ran. Her songs stirred sleeping seeds awake. Lovers wept with joy and ran off among the pear trees when she sang. Butterflies came and lit on her body like a dress. She smiled a mysterious half-smile as the wind spun veils around her—a cocoon—and she grew more and more into a woman waiting to emerge.

Primavera.

1. PARADISE

PRIMAVERA'S FIRST SONG

finding all the bunnerbuds
fossils and the procadillys
shine and glitter while we dance
spangles of the sea stars
the ocean fligs and flatters
but by any chance the mushroom grows
there is green moss under the heather
once again when biddle webs sleep
between the flowers
the green moss has grown
to be yellow and now all
the plants have grown
to be crystal
the trees glitter . . . green . . .

it is good for me and him

always to be in the grass lying down
feeling each other's warm
if you are a grownup
you can still
do anything
you can smell things
and look at things and
hear things upon your ears
while the wind always sings
for the pettler bug
all the rock flushed down
all of the water fountains
shook and the water
poured down
you can hear a white sugar moth
its strange curiosity
fills your mind while
birds fly about
butter scotches
and grass that hummers back

CALLIOPE

This was my daughter's first real song. She was
only three, but she sang it with such clarity and
strength that we all stopped what we were doing
to listen. I saw her father's dark eyes turn amber
with tears. He dropped the herbs he was harvest-
ing into the rushing water of the Sound where I

was washing our linens. He managed to whisper, "Who is this child you have brought into the world, Calliope? Where did she come from?"

I could have answered, "She came from an underworld of my sorrow, for that is where I gave birth to her. She came from a city of glass buildings and fireworks and champagne, for that is where I first carried her into the light. (And she loved light—always pointing her finger toward it with her eyes wonder-glazed, perhaps because she had first emerged in darkness.) She came from you, Dionisio, and that is why she has those sensual lips, dark-wave hair and flashing eyes. She came from you and me and also from the love of my brother Rafe and Paul, and that is why she loves music. But there is something else in this child that I can never explain. That is her very own soul, and it can sing."

But I did not say anything. We were all startled into silence: from the lips of my daughter came not only song; when Primavera sang, the flowers bloomed.

Should we have been surprised, we who brought back green to this Desert with our music, we who conquered fear and death with our love and music? Somehow this seemed different to us. Always before it had been something that all of us did together. It had not seemed like something we created from ourselves but a natural phenomenon that we helped into being. Yet here before us was magic. Primavera's magic spilled purely from her, and as she sang the hillside sprouted green shoots and then tight buds and from these we watched unfurl an orchestra of flowers.

I did not try to invade her thoughts. But as she grew I felt everything she felt, heard her in my mind. I know someday this will drive her away from us. I want to try to hold onto her forever, but how can I keep her from giving her gifts? Now it is as if she is imprisoned in a garden of her own making, lost in a tangle of redolent blossoms, and only when she has seen the cities without gardens will she know this place for what it is.

PRIMAVERA

I lived in paradise. That is what my parents told me. And my mother's brother, Rafe, and Paul.

"Believe me," Paul said, "I was restless, too. But you won't find better than this."

I inhaled the moist green-tinged air, the white-sweet feast of gardenias and the fruity red wine of the roses. Sunlight squinted through leaves onto my bare freckled shoulders.

Paul and I were sitting in the terraced garden under flowers so large that the petals were shelter from the sky. Iridescent birds sang like a strange fairy choir in trees drooping with nectar-full fruits. The grass bright as river.

I loved Paul as if he were my father, as if he were my brother. I loved him like a lover though he was years, years older. It was Paul who taught me to sing as I knelt at his feet in the terraced garden. Watching his face with the old scars on his cheeks, the perfect severe bones, the eyes so blue that they were not turquoise, aquamarine, cobalt, but all and none of these, his throat with the Adam's apple in motion. Sometimes it looked like it must hurt him to have that at his throat. I wanted one, too. Maybe if I were a boy he would love me.

A dark-haired quick boy like Rafe once was when Paul first fell in love with him. I look more like Rafe than like my own father. And how must this make Paul feel? Would he ever desire me because of that?

Paul is sculpted, pollen-gold; he is tall and bright like a candle.

"We live in paradise, Primavera."

"Then why is it called the Desert?"

"That is an old name. From the time before we came here. It was a real desert then." He pointed to the shelves of rock overgrown with foliage. "All that was just bare stone."

"Tell me about the other place," I said.

The city Paul came from, my father, my

mother, her brother, Rafe, whom Paul loves. None of them liked to talk about the city. It was called Elysia and they were *the* band there—Ecstasia. There were bright things in Elysia, not bright like here—stars—but blazing electric bright—the taste of brightness in your mouth, sweetness—not like here—the sweet of flowers—but a sweet taste of sugar like electric star fire. It was a carnival city. There were turning stages where you could ride carved horses and swans, glass palace bars where you could sip champagne until your blood became gold and luminous. It was a place where I could go to sing and be applauded, dress like a princess, crowned with diamond and ruby flowers.

They hated to talk about it, but sometimes I could get bits from my father, or from Paul when I charmed him enough with my voice. I would present him with a bouquet of flowers that appeared suddenly, opening and unfolding for him, and what could he do? He gave me something back—a story of a city of gloss and dazzle.

"They would love you there," he said. "But they would love you anywhere. A girl whose voice makes flowers bloom. But it's not worth it, Miss Spring."

He called me that—his spring.

"You fall under its spell, and then when you get old you go down below to an airless place to die. Like the Old Ones we brought back up when you were very small."

It was a story everyone repeated—how Paul and Rafe and my father had gone back to Elysia and rescued the Old Ones from the place called Under, bringing them back up and leading them into our paradise that is still called Desert.

"Now come sing for me," Paul said.

His own voice was older than he was. Ancient, unearthed from some mystical subterranean place, from his own Under, and also of the skies. People wept to hear him. The voice seemed to make his whole body ache. Maybe it made him bleed inside. I wondered if it hurt him, if it burned in his throat. He taught me the scale of notes. He shouted at me, "Again, again." I had to sing until I was weak. "You are a singer; you must sing." I sang and sang, giving him every kind of flower until I thought we would drown in them.

The flowers are suffocating. Sometimes I hate them. I long for jewel flowers, lilies encased in ice, glass roses. I long for mirrors instead of rivers, glass towers instead of these rocks.

Maybe the flowers will take over, strangling all of us.

Sometimes I dream that from the flowers emerge tiny women with veiny wings and pale greenish flesh, creatures who stuff pollen up my nostrils and prick my nipples with thorns until the tips bleed.

LOVE SONG

I know you will not be my lover
but I can't stop this waiting and perhaps
we were different flesh once radiant
in the sand and we traced our fingers
over the beads and amulets of white gold
jasmine stones and we were lost in each
    other's
long river hair
and maybe I was the man with huge glorious
    wrists
and you were a woman with fragile hips and
    shrouded eyes
and we bore a child and wandered wearing
    white robes
through the coral pink sands
a child together
a boy who swam in the
eye-blue water by the pink shore and came
    up dripping
with pearls and singing
and we wore palm leaf crowns
and ate the dates that split with sweetness
and later the bodies were one and in the
    tomb
the ashes sifted together and the selves' souls
    found other bodies
and so now when I see or hear you I am wild
to bury myself into you to be buried into

like a grave like a tomb like a garden
and my spirit remembers and shakes this new
   body
that is too small to contain the man's love
and I am overcome to be one

The day the stranger came, I heard the roar
and the children shrieking and I ran out of the
garden, to the top of the rock to see. The truck
was windowless and looked as if it would cut
your hand if you touched it. The door opened
and the stranger got out. His head was shaved
and he wore a cap. He looked up in my direc-
tion, his eyes flashing back light, and I was
afraid, but then I saw he wore mirrored lenses. I
wished I had his boots—thick black boots to the
knee with metal pieces at the toe. Paul might admire me in those boots.

Paul went to speak to the man. I could not
hear what they said, but I knew Paul was offering food, water, a place to sleep. All the Desert
people are kind to strangers. We always have
enough to share.

The man nodded his head. I saw that he had
almost no lips.

That night he was seated at our table under
the grape and wisteria bower. He still wore his
glasses, although the sky was turning as purple
as the fruits and flowers above our heads, but I

could feel him staring at me over the clusters of candles. He told us his name was Gunn.

"Don't you eat meat here?" he asked when we served him a plate of spiced fruit, nut butters, herbed rice, and honeyed bread.

"We don't eat meat," Paul said, as cool as I have ever heard him. "The animals are rare enough."

"I prefer my meat rare," the man Gunn said. He carefully cut away the insides of his bread with a knife from his pocket, leaving the crust. I could see my mother staring at the crust. She cannot bear waste.

"Where are you from?" asked Rafe, studying the man.

"Just south of here." I knew the eyes behind the lenses were on me. "One of the outposts before Elysia."

"Paul and I both grew up in one of the outposts," my father said. My father Dionisio is so open. I do not want to grow round and sleepy like he is, indulgent. I have always tried to become pure and hard like Paul.

One of Paul's eyebrows arched way up. But my father didn't see.

"They've changed a lot," said Gunn.

"Why have you come here?" Paul asked. He is not afraid to say what he thinks.

"I am selling some things," Gunn answered. This time he turned his head so everyone could see he was looking right at me. "I have a motor-cycle and a helmet and some boots. Things like that."

I felt as if he had looked right into me, at every organ. There was something grinding and almost mechanical-sounding about his voice.

"I don't think we have much use for those things out here," Rafe said, each syllable sharp. "We mostly stay where we are."

"Not all of you," the man said. "I heard some of you are adventurers. That you rescued a whole troop of Old Ones from Under once." His lipless mouth smiled.

There was silence at the table. I could see Paul's shoulders growing rigid. I wondered if Rafe would touch his arm under the table, trying to calm him.

"We don't need motorcycles out here," Paul said.

"Some of the young people might like to see what I have."

I lowered my head so no one would know what I was thinking. But I could feel my mother's mind pressing into mine. She's been able to read my thoughts since I was born. I wondered if I went far enough away, would her knowledge fade?

"Primavera," she said. "Will you help me with something?"

I had to go with her. As I stood up, the man's

mirrored eyes were fastening onto my breasts. I crossed the grass that looked almost blue with evening.

In the purple light of our tent, in the green rose incense smoke, my mother said, "I know you are thinking of leaving. I cannot stop you. But there are many dangers beyond the gardens we have made here."

"I know that." I could not disguise the anger in my voice.

"I can't help it that I can read your thoughts."

"I know."

"If you go away, I may not be able to anymore. Maybe that will be better for both of us. But also I won't be able to protect you."

"Mother, I haven't gone anywhere yet. Maybe you can't read my mind the way you think you can."

"Just be careful around that man," she said. She rubbed her temples the way she did when she was receiving one of her visions—one that she did not welcome.

Suddenly I felt a tenderness toward her well up in me. I could see how she was beginning to age. Part of me did not want to ever leave her. Since I was born, we spent all our time together. She wrote down the words I said, sang with me. She carried me in her arms through the Desert. I was never lonely; she knew every emotion I felt and what I needed. When I was older, we tended the flowers that sprang from our songs and cooked and ate the vegetables that flourished out of music. I remember the twilights, running over the damp grass till my feet stung, my ankles whipped with the cool blades, my mother chasing me, catching me in the deep softness of her arms and carrying me inside the tent, feeding me almond milk and bread and honey. I remember the mornings sitting on the stream bank singing up tall reedy flowers—irises, crocuses, laughing at the colors. I believed then that every child's mother could read her thoughts. Only as I grew older and began to have thoughts about Paul did it hurt me. She was always respectful; she never said that she knew how I felt about him. But I could sense it; I knew her concern and the heaviness of her love. Sometimes I couldn't breathe; it was like the suffocation of too much pollen.

I struggled to breathe all night. Finally, when my sweat had soaked through my nightgown and sleeping mat, I got up, wrapped myself in a sheet and went outside. My feverish feet felt cooled by the grass. I could see the stars. But I did not feel free. The blossom sweetness in the air was almost cloying. I knew my mother might wake at any moment and come looking for me.

Paul and Rafe slept in the blue tent. It was only a thin sheath of silky cloth that separated Paul from me—that and a world of longing that could never be traveled. Once, as a child, I had gone to him, suddenly out of breath in my parent's tent, then as tonight. I had thrown open the flaps and seen Rafe kneeling with Paul behind him. Paul's head was back and I could see the strain of his throat. He looked like a lion, like a god. He was all honeyed golden. Rafe is slender and dark-haired like me. They seemed to be hurting each other. Paul's voice sounded like glass splinters as he whispered some chant I could not understand. Neither of them saw me; their eyes were closed.

I ran away, but I never forgot what I had seen.

"Primavera," a man's voice said.

I jumped back and saw the stranger, Gunn, standing by his truck. He still wore the protective mirrors on his eyes, although the only light was from the stars.

"Would you like to see what I have to sell?" he asked me.

I felt ashamed, as if he had read my memory about Paul the way my mother could. I realized I was almost naked beneath my sheet and that my nipples were still raised from the memory, grazing the cloth of my nightgown.

I did not answer, but he had already brought the motorcycle out from behind the truck. It reminded me of a giant chrome and metal animal; in fact, between the handlebars was a horse's silver head. The horse's eyes were glittering mirrors and sharp teeth like nails were bared between thin metal lips.

"It's yours," he said. "It can take you anywhere. A girl like you needs to go somewhere she can be appreciated."

I narrowed my eyes at him. "How much?"

"Have you heard the expression, 'I got it for a song'?"

"You want a song?"

He nodded. "I've heard about you," he said. "How you make flowers grow by singing. I wanted to see for myself. I'm very interested in such . . . aberrations."

I started to turn away, but somehow I couldn't leave. I wanted that machine more than anything. It could take me everywhere.

"Just a song, Primavera. One of your little poems, really, aren't they? And real roses come out of the ground?" He lifted a pair of boots like his own, but smaller, out of the truck. The metal on the toes shone.

My tongue felt coated with a thin layer of iron. I wanted to spit at him.

"I can't sing for you," I said. I went back into my tent and lay in the darkness, thinking of the metal beast that could have taken me away from my family and Paul, all the way to Elysia.

But I cannot go long without singing. It is something that I must do every day. When I was a child, it was a praise for the morning and for the breath in my body that enabled me to sing. Later it became mourning for my loneliness. But I always sang.

The next day I was with Paul in our special garden. It is hard to find a place to sit. The vines have wrapped around everything and the flowers hang upside down—bells pouring out scent like music.

> *pink gloss taffeta*
> *beneath cascading light*
> *the wind shines and your eyes*
> *are gleam-water*
> *when you smash the sheet glass*
> *into webs*
> *the night shatters too*
> *I wear rhinestones like the fragments*
>
> *what matters except that we shine*
> *like taffeta in the strange river light of*
> *   drugged houses*
> *candles in pink smoked glass*
> *our teeth are sharpened to points and we*
> *   suck*
> *white wine*
> *they cut everything—our teeth*

I sang Paul waxy yellow and harsh pink flowers that looked like twisted birds. Paul examined their fierce beaklike faces.

"What is wrong, Miss Spring?" he asked. "That song came from someplace else."

We turned at the same time and saw the man, Gunn, standing in the shadow of a rock.

"Very pretty," he said. "Why do you think you know how to do that?"

"I think you should leave." Paul moved closer to him.

"I have never heard of a Desert man talking to anyone like that. I thought you welcomed everyone here."

"Not everyone."

"Have you ever seen a centaur, Mr. Desert?"

I could feel Paul clenching.

"You know, half human, half animal? I call them Mutants. Aberrations. But some aren't that obvious. There are also the men who have sex with men. They're half male, half female, in a way. What do you think about that?"

"Get out of here," I said. This time I was really ready to spit, to pull off that little smug cap and those mirror eyes.

"It was a very pretty song," he said. "Thank you for giving it to me. Now I'll have to fulfill my promise."

And before Paul or I could say anything, he had disappeared back into the lands beyond our Desert. All that remained of him was the bitter taste on the back of my tongue and the gifts I found later.

* * *

I was taking a walk along the Sound, the river that people say came rushing when my parents and Paul arrived here, found Rafe, and played their music. How strange to imagine this place without water. An empty ravine of sand. I would have been so different if I grew up in that Desert. Perhaps my passions would not be so lush and grasping then.

It was dark, but the light of the planets touched the water so that the foam and bubbles shone frothy white, glancing stars back up at me. Where the water pooled, stilled in places and more shallow, pink, white, yellow, and blue water lilies, with flat green pads large enough to sit on, floated. My mother calls them nymph flowers, and when I was little my father used to tease me and say they found me inside of one. In the moonlight, there was something ominous about the nymph lilies as if they were calling me to them. And then they might reach out stalks from beneath the water, encircle me and bring me back to them. Maybe I was born among those dense wet clusters.

Sometimes I dream of strange creatures dripping wet and shimmering with iridescent scales, spitting pearls at me and reaching out with clammy silvered fingers.

* * *

I followed the river to the cave where I go when I need to be alone, where I dream of palaces of marble and crystal. I have never told anyone—not Paul, no one—about this place, though my mother probably knows about it. I parted the vines that drape the entrance and slipped inside.

And there, hidden in the dim, cool, smooth cavern where no leaves or flowers grow, something gleamed. What could have lit it? Maybe some trick of the moonlight on the water outside reflected back through the cascading vines. Or the brightness of my own eyes as I sensed freedom. In the depths of the cave there was a helmet, small men's boots, and the motorcycle with the horse's head.

I left them there, but I knew I would return.

The ritual of the burning tree.

We gathered around the chosen one. I felt my feet going down into the earth, layers of darkness crumbling away, my arms extending, hands heavy with poems like over-ripe fruit. I knew I would soon be barren again. I would sing and be left empty like a tree picked clean. Or a tree burned.

The night was black. The fire red. The tree green. The ashes will be white.

The Mother and the Father stood holding hands in their black robes, sharing the cup of wine. The Magician had his red torch. The Gardener held his vessel of water, a wreath of green herbs on his head. Who was I in white? The Maiden? I wished I was the Warrior. Then I would have ridden away from here. But I was as immobile and at the mercy of the others as the fruit tree.

Our circle was incomplete. There was no King to take me in his arms, uproot me from this binding earth so that I could dance away with him. I wanted the Magician to be my King, but he was lost chanting mysteries, his eyes ice sapphires when I came too close. There was no Spirit Guide to take me to my King, no ancient Crone to protect me out in the wilderness. There was no Child Spirit for me to hold.

And there was no Demon. In paradise we won't allow there to be any demons. But they exist. Maybe part of me wished the man Gunn was there so that my family would be reminded. We are not complete here, pretending the darkness is always full of fireflies and that all that hides beneath the earth are seeds waiting to be flowers.

We all began to sing and Magician knelt and touched the torch to the tree. I could feel the heat crackling too near. I smelled singed hair instead of leaves and imagined that beneath the song a tree was wailing, not knowing she was a sacred offering, not understanding the reason for her death.

As my hair went up in flames, I woke.

* * *

We had a festival to celebrate the full moon. The women wore flowers and gathered on the rocks. We played music. I had some bells tied to my wrists, but I did not sing. I was about to bleed and my abdomen felt swollen, engorged.

The men came walking out of the distance from the other side of the Sound. I saw Paul with his guitar. He was the tallest of the men. He held his back so straight and his feet were planted in the grass with each step. His eyes were half closed, the moonlight touching on his cheekbones. Rafe was beside him playing a drum.

We danced on opposite sides of the water as the moon rose higher. I stood across from Paul. He did not look directly at me, but I felt his music inside of my body as if he were playing my organs like instruments.

The men waded out into the water. Some of the women tied up their skirts and joined them. I knotted my dress between my thighs and splashed in. I wished I had worn my men's tunic, but my mother had told me to wear the dress. The water came up to my calves and was cold. Stones knocked and cut my ankles. I wanted to catch the moonbeams—lock them in a lantern or wreathe my hair with some. I skimmed my palms over the surface and lifted my empty hands up.

In Elysia, the bright things would be hard and real.

I looked at the moon. She seemed to be mocking me, saying, "My beams are not yours to harvest." The water chuckled. White moths trembled in my hair.

Paul did not go into the water. He stood on the bank with his guitar. I danced in front of him and I felt that he was playing for me. My damp dress clung to my breasts and my stomach. I wished again I had worn the heavy tunic that hid my shape. I was afraid I might start to bleed.

After the moon was high, we all dried off by a huge camp fire in a clearing and ate. There were tables spread with food—grains in painted bowls, vegetables on plates of leaves, tureens of fragrant soup, baskets of edible flowers and fruits, large sculptural breads. There was even wine.

My father was leaning against a tree, drinking. He looked heavy. My mother says he used to be leaner than Paul.

I went over to him. We hardly talked anymore. For a moment, I thought, maybe I can tell him about Paul. Maybe he could help me. I remembered how close we had been when I was a child. We were always laughing about something; I was always running into his arms. But now it seemed he didn't know what to say to me.

"In Elysia they drink every night," he said. I

could tell by his voice he was missing the city.

"Can I talk to you about something?" I asked.

He took a gulp of wine from his bowl. "Are you having a good time?"

I shrugged and looked at the group of people dancing in a circle, thrusting back their heads and raising their arms to the sky.

"You haven't been dancing. When you were a little girl, we used to dance with you standing on my feet. Remember?"

"I need another partner now."

"I guess I really am an Old One," my father said.

"What?"

"Oh, nothing. It's Elysia talking."

I couldn't tell him about my feelings for Paul or any man. All he could think about was how I wasn't his baby now. And even though he was not a man afraid of love or lust, I knew he couldn't accept those feelings in his child.

He refilled his bowl and grabbed my mother's waist from behind. His face looked wild as he pulled her into the dark, soft leaves, out of the circle of crisp firelight, and I turned away.

My dress dried off; it smelled of pine, water, and wood smoke. I drank a large bowl full of wine. I felt the sweetness sinking into my knees. I felt the nectar of my body dripping down like the wine dripping into my mouth.

I wandered back down to the water. Paul was

sitting on a rock by himself, playing his guitar. His long legs hung down the sides of the rock and the guitar was nestled against his narrow hip.

I climbed up and sat beside him. The rock still felt warm from the day. I lay down, pressing my blood-filled belly to the hard heat. Paul played his song. After awhile I sat up and looked at him from behind the strands of hair that had fallen into my eyes.

"Paul?"

"Yes, Miss Spring."

I wanted to ask him to hold me in his arms. I clutched my wrist, feeling the pulse in the vein. My breasts swelled. I was afraid of them. I was choked with my secret love. I felt sick and burned with love.

Maybe it is not love. Maybe it is only my own hollowness. But I want to believe it is also love, a love that comes from dreams of a bright rain like fire in an ashen field and white horses that run through my throat like tears and roses burning my breasts and rose quartz cooling my breasts and the bird that sings all day and all night in the silver birch tree.

"I love you, Paul," I whispered.

He said, "I know." That was all. His voice sounded chilly and far away.

"I mean, I love you. I want to be with you."

He did not look at me. Then I saw his shoulders shrug.

I realized what I had done. I stumbled to my feet and scrambled down the steep side of rock, falling onto the grass. Some flowers sprinkled me with moisture. Blood and wine stirred in my belly. I listened for his voice calling me back, but all I heard was the taunting festival music.

I ran through the crowd of dancers to the edge of the clearing. Torches were flaring and I felt like one of them with my stiff body and my burning face. Someone caught my arm. Was it Paul? I was still hoping even then. But it was Rafe. Ashamed, I tried to hide myself from him.

"Where are you going?"

"Let go of me."

"Primavera, what is it?"

I struggled to wrench my wrist away. We really did resemble each other. But not enough, I thought. Not in the ways that matter to Paul.

"Listen," he said, "we've all felt it. Loss. We all understand."

"What are you talking about?" I was furious. Had he overheard me speaking to Paul? Had my mother told him my secret? Did he just know? I hated him. I hated them all.

He let go of me and I ran away from there, away from them, across the water, through the field.

I ran all the way back to my secret cave. The

motorcycle was still there. I lay on the grainy dry dirt beside it all night. In the morning, my dress was covered with red stains.

If I could make the blood stop forever I would do it. The story of Paul's cold eyes was written in red between my thighs. It smelled of iron and the underworld.

I jumped in the river and ran home soaking wet. My mother came out of the tent.

"Where were you?" she shouted.

"Don't you know? You always know where I am and what I do."

"You should have told us. We were worried. Paul said you just ran off."

"Why should I tell you anything? You push inside my head all the time."

She looked haggard. I could see what time was doing to her.

"I never try to go where I am not wanted. Last night I didn't know where you were."

"But you tried."

"We were afraid you had hurt yourself."

"Leave me alone. Stay out of my head."

But I knew she could not as long as I was this close to her.

I did not tell my family that I was going. I left them a note saying I would be back someday and not to look for me.

I stand looking at myself in the lake this dawn.

My hair hangs down to my waist in thick dark twists that my mother calls elf-locks. I am trying to pin it up, fit it under the helmet. My skin is light brown and freckled. My eyes are flashes of dark in the lake, my nose is sharp, my cheekbones broad and high. I have narrow boyish hips that I am proud of, boyish legs in the big black men's boots, but my breasts are full. I have wrapped them in linen so I will look more like a young boy. I have the motorcycle the stranger Gunn gave to me in exchange for my flowers.

What do I know about life? I don't think I know very much about anything.

These are the things I know. When I sing flowers grow. They may choke me. Sometimes I want to cut them all down, chop their stems as if I am cutting my own vocal chords. I have a motorcycle, a helmet, and heavy black boots. I have a flask of Sound water, some loaves of bread, some nuts and dried fruits. I love Paul, but he will never love me. The world is not here.

CALLIOPE'S VISION

You are walking in a field beside a lake. There are plum trees, fig trees, uncut grass littered with bird-pecked fruit. Thin red roses drift. You look into the water.

Suddenly the dawn is still. Even the leaves,

that have up to this moment been shifting in a kind of frenzy, wild with the wind, freeze.

A horse is grazing—a huge white horse all haunch and stride. It looks up and comes over to you, nibbling thorny roses. You look into the vast and gazing eyes. You see how huge its irises are, see the heft and sway of thick white haunch, the momentous curve of life. The horse lets you stroke its nose—a tremble of little hairs. It stands gazing and still with a kind of pleasure, sometimes extending its lips and teeth to nibble the thin red roses.

Everything is so still. Only this creature flicking its tail and blinking its lashes, licking your hand with its rough wild-rose tongue. Then it turns and runs back through the trees, cutting a path of pale light.

You are leaving us. And as you move out into the world, what I feared and what you wish for is becoming real: I no longer see your face.

PAUL

Dearest Spring.

When you were a baby I felt almost as if you were my own. This may sound strange to you, but because you looked so much like your mother's brother I truly imagined that if he and I had been able to have a child you would be ours. I heard you sing and knew that you were like my daughter. When I was young I sounded a little like that, putting words together as if they were bright beads or sweets.

You grew and I was amazed at your beauty. It almost frightened me at times. I didn't want you to come too near. I have never felt for women like this, but when I saw you calling up the sunflowers, I felt my heart beat as it does for Rafe. This I can never tell you.

But you have left us so I write these words in secret.

Some people call me a magician because of the music I can make. But I am unable to do the simplest things. I wish that I had been able to tell you how beautiful I think you are, especially that night on the rock, how your songs have brought back all the tenderness and yearning of my life. I am not one who can easily express love; this has been my grief.

In the outside world, where all that is good can perish, please treasure what you must know in your heart is your family's love for you. And my love for you. Because I believe that you knew it despite everything.

Be safe for us.

RAFE

I don't blame her for leaving.

At her age, I would probably have done the same thing. I loved the stage and the heat of lights giving me a halo—like the one Paul always seems to have—when I was beating my drums. I loved the girls and boys watching me and the feeling of reaching inside of them with my music. I loved Elysia and would have wanted it even if I'd been born in this place. I felt immortal then.

But that changes fast.

I know Primavera loves Paulo. Why shouldn't she? Even though he's a lot older than she is, Paul is a beautiful man. His voice makes people leave their bodies. Or maybe possess their bodies for the first time. He is like some kind of beacon. A fire on a hill. The sun. Why wouldn't you fall in love with the sun if he were a man with blue eyes and fierce tender hands? And you were a young girl who could make flowers sing and had never been out of her own tiny garden?

I saw how Paul looked at her and it was strange, because for as long as I've known him I've never seen him look at anyone but me that way.

I've always looked. Men and women. I can't help it. Restless. I'm a speed-child even now that

I'm on my way to becoming an old man. But Paulo? It hurt me. I never said anything. I won't.

I remember when I was in love for the first time with Lily in Elysia and Paul never said a word. He was mean sometimes, cruel even, but only to keep himself distant, not to come between us. When Lily died, Paul mourned her as if he had loved her, as if it were Paul who had sacrificed everything to bring her back from the dead in his mind for those moments. He wrote songs that expressed my sorrow with such truth that it almost terrified me. But he is Paul—of course he'd be able to do that. So now I can try to hold him while he worries about our Spring.

And I worry too, though I won't tell Callie. I'll tell Paul and Dionisio and Callie, "She'll be all right. We would all probably have gone on a journey if the only thing we knew was here. Besides, she was born in Elysia, remember? That desire is already in her. But she'll be back. We all came away from there finally."

But I worry. I worry because she is young and slender and beautiful and holds a great gift and because she is my sister's child and because she is the only person I know who feels for Paulo the same passion I feel. I only hope she finds what she is looking for and returns to us—whatever that may mean for me and Paul.

DIONISIO

My daughter has become a woman now and it's like I don't even know her anymore. I don't know how to talk to her. She's a mystery.

She looks at me and her eyes are cold. When she was little, she was crazy about me. We always laughed together. She let me dance with her. She brought me flowers and stuck them in my hair. Now I think she thinks I am foolish or even disgusting. The only one she likes to talk to is Paul. I think she wishes I was more like him. I have gotten fat and slow. But she's changed, too. She used to come to me with all her little songs and stories.

"The small fort mermaid was very happy since she lived in a castle in the ocean. She was popping up some mornings. She came to a dark place. It had sea-pines, pies, cakies, and pigs. She had friends and biggest snails, flowers, turtles, diamonds, rocks, and the biggest biggest sand wich and lived in sheets of gold. A small people crept in the bottom of the ocean and her bed. The small people laughed to see the mermaid cuddling down in her bed. The mermaid was happy to see the people.

"I'm going to give these poems to people," she would say.

She would sing:

I dance papa
I'm dancing
I'm dancing up hills evermore
I love my heart I can dance
la la la la la la
I have to dance
I have a flute evermore
I love to sing and dance

When Paul told her about the ocean he used to surf in, she said, "Deep below the longness bumps up into big ruffles like a heart that makes the sea bubble."

When I cried because her songs were so beautiful she kissed my tears. "Don't cry, Papa." She stared at her reflection in my eyes. "The little dolls in your eyes are getting wet. Mama, Papa is tanged with tears."

She sang:

the girl walked among the plump sugar stars
and the asterdart lambs all flew along
with bells and golden chariots

there is no living horse
there is no copper horse
there is no glass horse
there is a leather horse
and that was what it was and Rainia was the
    name of her

*in the palace where gold was hung and a
  beast spoke through a mirror*

Maybe mystery fragments remembered from another life? Or premonitions? Calliope wrote everything down.

Now Primavera has left us. But the baby girl child who loved me left a long time before.

2. NEVERLAND

PRIMAVERA'S JOURNEY

The motorcycle is large and powerful between my gripping thighs. I have left the green that has bathed my eyes for as long as I can remember. Now the road runs through banks of sand and looming rocks.

I tell myself to breathe. The stern stone faces with their gaping jaws and sockets remind me of the giants I dreamed of as a child—huge, crushing things numbing my limbs with their gaze.

The rocks where we live are covered with green and bright yellow moss and water spills down them; reeds and flowers grow in the crevices. But these rocks are naked, scowling. For a moment I think I will sing, leaving a trail of color as I pass, but my song would wither in the case of this helmet, the motorcycle engine would drown out my voice, and there is something about the barren landscape that I want. Perhaps it will purify me, dry up the yearning inside of me.

Something in the air makes me gasp and recoil even beneath my helmet. What is that horror? It is a stench of death. I know this even before I see the place at the side of the road. It is fenced in—a death camp. Rows and rows of cattle stand pressed together under the hot sun. They sweat fear. Their eyes stare out blindly, past the jagged-jawed skulls mounted on stakes, toward the road. But I must pass them without stopping, without singing to them. What good would it do them—although they have probably never grazed in a lush green field and eat only the rough yellow weeds and powders they are fed. But I can't sing when I see them, smell them. I have heard of this place. The cattle will be slaughtered and sold for meat. This is their life—caged and awaiting death. I think I imagine them calling to me, "Go back, go back where you came from." But I am always dreaming strange unreal things.

Now the air smells sharp, tastes salty as sweat. I hear thunder.

It is not coming from the sky but from below, and as I round the bend in the road I see beneath the cliffs an expanse of water that seems to go on forever.

I have heard tales of the sea. Paul and Rafe used to ride the waves. That was when it was still clean enough. Even then they said it made their eyes burn and sometimes gave them rashes on their skin.

I always imagined Paul lifted on the curl of a wave that is like some giant dissolving flower. It was hard to imagine that much water and it was hard to think of Paul in water at all. I see him always as dry, hot, white light.

But now the sea is before me. I stop on the edge of a cliff and look down. These waters are not like the waters of the Desert; you can see through those streams to the glittering sand of their beds and you can even hear how clear they are. This body of water is heavy and deep and swollen with mysteries. Its voice is full of turbulence and sorrow.

I leave my bike hidden behind a rock and half walk, half slide down a steep incline. Brittle brambles tear at my skin and pebbles slip churning beneath my feet. I am not drawn to this ocean as I thought I might be. It is unclean and wild. But I keep scrambling toward it anyway.

The beach is deserted beneath a gray sky. The waves heave themselves onto the black-streaked sand. I look out at the horizon, wondering what Paul must have felt as he ran down toward the water and thrust himself in. If I did that—even if it wasn't boiling with toxins—I would be pulled under. I would drown with the water seeping into my mouth, nose, and eyes. I do not have his impenetrability.

Paul and Rafe probably sat on a beach like this one, looking out at the waves, dreaming of clear water. They kissed on a beach, while their bodies still seemed to rock with the rhythm of the ocean.

The wind lifts the heavy locks of my hair and swirls them around my face. Through these darker waves I watch those others. Paul told me that once a long time ago the oceans were the colors of our waters, only more brilliant, more like the precious stones in Elysia. He said that they were full of leaping fish and that the sands were white and scattered with giant rainbow shells.

"When I rode the waves," he said, "I would try to imagine what it was like then. But I never thought we could have what we have now."

He is so content in paradise. Why can't I be? I have left our place of enchantment to see a wound of water.

No sign of life except clouds of stinging flies. I walk down the shore, my boots digging against little shelves of sand so that the shelves crack and spill.

Something is lying at the edge of the water. It

looks like a pile of seaweed and debris but I get closer; I see the flies swarming around a fish tail.

So there are fish here? But no, something is wrong. Closer still. The limp, scaled tail connects not to a fish's head but to the bloated white torso of a woman. Her face is blanched, cheeks sunken, neck strangled with strands of salt-encrusted slimed weed. A sticky pale substance quivers across her breasts. Her eyes stare at me from a pooling glaze of salt.

The dead mermaid reminds me of that in myself which would keep me wanting and lifeless, all of the things that would repel Paul. I hate her for lying there imprisoned even in death by her own animal part. And I hate myself for hating her. And for leaving home.

If this mermaid swam in the waters of our Desert she would be alive. She would have plunged from a flowery rock into the sheen and sparkle of the Sound, unfurling her tail, tossing greenish-golden hair, trembling with pleasure. And once the sea was all dazzling and pure. I wonder if now the Desert is the only unpoisoned place.

I have left the dead mermaid and the sea.

Here the sky is full of fumes and drizzle. We know rains that are fresh as our Sound, drops we catch on our tongues and splash our faces with, but this rain is stagnant water, and when I make the mistake of tasting it I spit out bitter ash and worse.

I have gone inland to a body of water across which lies a cluster of buildings—a city, but this is not Elysia.

The water is black and bubbling and so thick that the huge chunks of broken bridge float on top like phantom barges. And some are boats now. Skinny dirty children dressed in rags sit on the boats, pushing through the mire with oars made from scraps of wood. They are going back to where they live.

All I see of it is the husks of burned buildings black against the evening sky and the smoke rising up from sulfur bonfires. I wonder why the children are going back there. Maybe the desert frightens them even more than that place. Some are running along the shore shouting and waving sticks. Some have found rocks or bones. One holds up a small white object—the intricate skull of a bird—and moves the hinge of its jaw, making squawking sounds.

"Intruder," caws the bird skull, the scrawny boy's puppet. He and some others run over to me, not too close, and stand staring at me and my bike. I must look like someone from another planet to them.

Their eyes are huge with hunger. I take off my helmet, shaking my hair free, and say, "I'm looking for Elysia."

"This isn't it," the largest child snarls.

They are moving in closer like an army, smelling of swamp. They are missing teeth, but the ones left in their mouths have been filed to sharp points.

I do not know what else to do, so I start to sing.

elves elves elves
all threading their clean silver
around me in a web
tell them I will come down to the dark road
they give me wings like lit rain
I say dance dance dance with me for I have
    reaped
the harvest it hangs jewelled in my eyes and
    richly against my breast
it hangs red and sugar-glossed and
    poisonous
at my earlobes
but you will want it in your dark glades
where water rushes through the moss
    violets
tell the eldritch man whose face is lit from
    deep
that I will bring him lilies and lie with him
in those bough arms
I will cry out from the crystal-encrusted
    caves to him

for he is of the old race the sea deep
  marbled race
who have found jewels of rain and light
in the pillared hall
we hang garlands and wear wreaths of
  candles
we dance where it is dark in our snail-
  silvered robes
night night come through the mirror
with your drugs that paint red lace on the
  white walls
with your bundle of nasturtiums and violets
cut out the pain that lodges like a gnarled
  white root
in my rib cage
the birds cry out shattering the mirrors of
  night
and a rose deepens out of the rose
spreading across the watercolor wash
like paint meeting the wet surface

Before I know it, not roses but angry, acrid, yellow sunflowers have sprouted out of the humus and garbage piles along the bank. They turn their heads, the brown globes of their eyes seeking sun, but here the sky is gray and the flowers look dizzy and lost, as if asking me, Where are we? What have you done to us?

But the children are ecstatic. They leap around the sunflowers, yanking them from the ground, ripping the roots. I feel the violent shredding inside of me. The children fight over the seeds and try to nibble the petals but spit them out. I wish I had been able to sing up some carrots and potatoes for them.

The first boy seems to have taken command. "She's one of the Fairies."

This silences the whispers running among them. They look solemn.

"Are you a Fairy?"

"Do you live in the Garden?"

"She must be; look at her skin and her teeth. She's too pretty for humans."

"Come back with us."

"Come to our city."

Suddenly they are looking at me in a different way, mesmerized, awed, even. They are all so thin and dirty. What would Paul do? He would go with them.

"Will my bike fit on your boat?" I ask.

"What do you think?" says one boy proudly. "Our boats are strong enough to carry all of us, rocks and bike."

One of the littlest boys catches my attention. His shoulders are narrow and stooped and he mostly looks at his feet, but when I catch him looking up at me I see his eyes have a softness, a liquid melt of blue. He has a high forehead, and it looks even more so because his pale little skull is bald.

"Just for a little while," I say. "I have to get to Elysia."

RIVER

I heard of Fairies from my Mama but now my Mama's gone. I wish my Mama could see this Fairy cause she is all sparkly looking and when she sang the song about those creatures the big Flowers all grew up right there out of the dirt.

She—Fairy—has a big motorbike with a Horse Head on it. I read about a Horse. I like to pretend Mama and I are in a big green place and the Horse pressing his soft paddy nose into our hands and not afraid of Mama like the People are. Were.

My Mama's gone now. And we were never in any big green place and I never really saw a Horse.

I bet Fairy saw a real Horse. I bet she lives in the Garden where all the Flowers grow. When I get back to Library I am going to look up about those Flowers Fairy made. I'll have to remember what they looked like real well. I didn't pull them out of the ground like the others did.

Library is my favorite place. Maybe I can bring Fairy there. And maybe she can show me the Flower she made grow in one of my big favorite Books.

I've looked Mama up in those Books but she's not there. There's Woman and there's Bird but nothing like the two of them together that I could find. Except this thing called Harpy but that's not Mama. Ugly and Foul they call her and that makes me hate my big favorite Books so that must not be her.

I watch Fairy sitting in the boat. Maybe she will be like my Mama now.

NEVERLAND

The barge takes us across the murky water. A group of children sit huddled in the belly of the boat, staring at me as we go. I take a loaf of bread out of my pack and they devour it, tearing off big hunks and shoving it into their mouths. They don't let the little bald boy have any. He looks mournful. His eyelashes are long and feathery.

I wonder how this boat will ever get us to the other side. And what will happen if it doesn't. This is not water you want to swim in.

But we get to the shore. The children all scramble off and I follow with my bike. I look around at the streets heaped with garbage and the sky that is black now. We go through a cement tunnel covered with graffiti scrawls. People lie heaped together. I can see their eyes in the darkness.

We start up a steep hill. Small bonfires burn in dirt pits—some surrounded by people with bluish complexions, others abandoned. The buildings lining the streets were once maybe little palaces with wide-angled windows, turrets, carvings. You can see the remains of pastel paint in some places through the layers of grime and the angry black letters—"HOWL," "WHY ARE WE HERE," "PANIC," "MEAT," "NEVERLAND." Now most of the windows are shattered and it looks as if things have been ripped from the architecture. Here a cherub without a face or a single stone lion beside the empty pedestal that once supported . . . what?—its missing partner.

The children see a featherless pigeon waddling in the gutter and take off after it. They shout and throw the stones they have collected. One rock hits the wheeling bird and the children form a circle around it so I cannot see what they are doing—only hear the glut of thudding and then ripping sounds. My stomach feels like the tortured bird. The children find a free bonfire and dangle the raw pieces over the flame. Only the littlest bald-boy stays back, shivering. He must be so hungry.

When the feast is over, we walk on. One boy is picking pieces of gristle from between his filed teeth. The blue-eyed boy stays close to me, his feet turned slightly in.

Some gray weeds in a windowbox—the only foliage—must remind the children because they all start to shout, "Sing to us! Sing to us!"

I feel the tightness in my throat. I don't want to sing anymore. I am weak and tired. Wondering why I have come here.

Seized with the impulse to escape. I remember the children's teeth and think of the pummeled and torn bird. But what else could they do living in this place? They have not grown up beside a giving river with fruit trees on its banks.

I leap on my bike and kick it to life. For a moment the sound startles the children, and they draw back in time for me to pull off down the street.

There are no cars driving, only motionless ones, rusted out and gutted, where some people have made their homes. Faces peer out the back windows at me—sometimes whole families stuffed inside. The streets are steep and the landscape does not change—everywhere the same burned-out buildings and piles of filth. I wonder what I should do, if I should try to return to the river and find a boat.

Then I hear the soft voice—a slight lisp, a slight whistle.

"You can stay with me."

I turn around and there behind me on the bike, holding on to the seat so he does not give himself away by touching me, is the bald boy with the sweet blue eyes.

"Don't be mad."

I smile at him.

"Where to?" I say.

The streets get steeper and wind darkly—the buildings more cramped together. Here and there a toothless man or woman, faces aged to express the skull beneath the skin, stands with a cart full of what look like weeds or strange gelatinous pancakes. The most crowded place is a stall with a cage where pigeons stumble, bumping beaks in a stupor. A barely legible sign reads "YES THESE ANIMALS TO EAT NOT FOR PETS." I wonder if anyone here would think otherwise. The sign must be very old, kept as a reminder of some past when that was a possible question. Then I see another cage—this one full of mangy dogs. The eyes are pleading and human.

People kill the birds right on the streets, slitting their throats with pocket knives. There are pools of fresh blood and dried pools of blood. Dirty heaps of speckled feathers. The bonfires burn, roasting the limbs and breasts and wings. Animal smell. Charred smell. I hear a dog's scraping yelp.

The little boy behind me reaches out, pointing, then puts his tiny chilly hands around my waist. "Go that way."

We drive down a hill past more of the decaying buildings. Some of them remind me of the bread houses my mother and I used to make to resemble the buildings she remembered from Elysia, covered with a frosting of pastel petals, but bread houses smashed in and nearly ruined, trash heaped on the street in front of them.

At the end of a long stretch of houses we get to an expanse of barren land. Dead trees lie on their sides, their roots exposed and raw. Clouds of dust fill the air.

"This is our Garden," whispers my passenger.

I glance back at him. He is still holding on to me. The dust is making his eyes water. He points down into the "garden" and I go that way. There are no people to be seen.

The building looks strange standing in the center of all this nothingness. It is the skeleton of a glass palace; a few panes still tremble in their frames, but most have shattered. Still I can see the delicate form of the dome, the curved walls that must once have glistened, let in starlight and green-tinted sunlight, if there was ever starlight and sunlight here.

"This is where I live."

I stop the bike and we get off. The boy is looking up at me. He sucks his lower lip.

"You can come in," he says.

I follow him inside the fragile structure. I can hear the tinkling sound of glass. For a moment I think I smell the ghost of flowers, but very faint, a pale hint of night violet from very far away. Then it is gone. I must have imagined it. How cold it is. Colder even than outside. There are broken pieces of pottery and troughs of dirt everywhere.

"You live here alone?"

He nods. "No one else will come into the Garden. They think it's haunted. And too cold here anyway." He wipes his nose on his sleeve.

"But you?"

"I like to be alone. I play that the Flowers live here with me."

"What's your name, little one?"

"River."

"That's a perfect name for you."

He shuffles his feet. "What's your name, Fairy?"

"Primavera."

He looks puzzled. Then he says, "Fairy, why did you leave your Garden?"

I suddenly see Paul's face. This child's skin is so smooth, almost poreless, his little face so soft, but there is something about his eyes that reminds me of how Paul's must have been once. Why did I leave? I left all that beauty and love. That garden for this one.

"I'm not sure, River. I guess because I wanted an adventure. And to escape something that hurt me, but it seems far away now."

"Have you been to a lot of places?"

"Not yet."

"Have you seen a lady with . . . " His voice trails off and he sucks his lip again.

"Who? Are you looking for someone?"

He weaves his fingers together.

"River, do you have a mother and a father?"

"I had a Mama, but the man came and took her away."

"What man?"

But River doesn't want to talk anymore. He takes my hand and leads me through the cold cobwebby building. This is where he lives alone. He does not say another word, only whistles softly like a small bird-boy in his cage of glass.

RIVER

Today I took Fairy to Library. She loved it. She says in the Garden there aren't nearly so many Books—that everyone has to write everything down by hand on special parchment and it takes a long time. There are some old printed Books she says but not as many as here.

We stayed all day in Library reading. We found a place where not too many people are curled up sleeping on the floor and not too many boys throwing things and running down the long tables covered with knife marks. It's way up in the stacks and warm. It's kind of dark but enough light comes through the little window shaped like a round glass Rose. I told Fairy I sleep here when my house gets too cold, but mostly I stay in my house because I like to be alone.

Library has high marble ceilings and echo floors and windows like glass Flowers. The best thing though is the Books. Fairy asked how come if all these people sleep here and run wild over the tables how come there are still any Books left. I say because most people don't know how to read and the ones that do love Books too much to take them away forever. That would be a terrible thing. How do you know how Fairy asks. To read. I tell her my Mama taught me when I was really little and I keep teaching myself more.

I chose one of my big favorite Books. The one called EXTRA To GAMB. I look up FLOWER and show Fairy the pictures of all the little parts. Sepal Stamen Pistil Filament. I show her the word Inflorescence. I think it is a pretty sounding word. Fairy does, too. She says that words are special, magic even.

Fairy chose a Book of Poems. It is a little old Book with the front cover missing but the binding is all thick and bumpy with gold and the edge of every page is gold. I don't know a lot of the words in it but I like the Pictures. Every certain number of pages there is a really thin piece of paper like a skin and under it is a beautiful little Painting to go with the Poems. Pale floaty ladies draped in robes sitting on Flowery banks, Green Fields, Water, Trees, Blue Skies full of Clouds, and shivers of Birds. There is one of a lady in a pale green robe with big pink Wings on her back and a wreath of Birds all around her. It reminds me a little of Fairy because of the long wavy vines of hair and it reminds me of Mama. Fairy says it is a Picture of Morning. Mama had Wings too so maybe Mama was Morning. I want to whisper to Fairy that Mama had Wings and that I got born out of an egg and tell her about the feathers that grow out of my head but I don't tell her yet. Fairy says the Poems were written so very long ago by a man who could make magic with the words he wrote.

After Library Fairy sings up some sticky blue Flowers out of the mud outside. She makes a face and says they aren't the best she's ever done. I say I think they are pretty. We take them to one of the old women who sells food. I'm afraid Fairy will buy the tiny speckled eggs or even worse one of the live pigeons, but instead she gets some clear noodles and some buns. We go back to my house and build a fire and eat. Then Fairy sings me to sleep. I dream I am inside her song and that the glass house is full of Inflorescence.

PRIMAVERA

Birches

roses once clogged my throat
but I wished for
birch trees in my fingertips
peeling white bark almost silver
the color of mist
if you scrape birch bark with your nail
it squeaks and peels soft like ash
I would like to make a fire of birch bark
I wonder if it would be a silver fire
leaf eyes and silver manes in it

we could visit the gnomes under the birch
   roots
under the birches
gnomes are the ones with warm dens and
   lovely fires
and shiny copper soup kettles and roasted
   apples and many children
giants are those other ones

when I was little or now
when I am afraid, they are there
I don't ever really see them
sometimes I am them
my hands are thick thick encased in thick
my body is heavy heavy impossible

sometimes I just feel them on me or above
   me crushing
I can never explain
it is the numb fat sinking of anxious sleep
I can never explain

the fairies are not sleep like that

the fairies are some other thing

they are the rare lights up in the leaves
they are what it is like to dance when you
   are hungry
I think all their faces are pinched from not
   eating
and from chills caught when they sleep in
   the dew
they have no breasts and you can see their
   ribs
when I am with them I am green and fragile
   and hungry
and pinched looking
I am happy in a strange green way
the marsh gases sweep up from the dark
   reeds like poison
and hang suspended
little lights flash beneath the marsh gas
mushrooms and water lilies grow thick and
   wet and pale
fairies are the way lights reflect in water
the way oil turns to rainbows

birch fingers catching mist

don't ask me about the elves
I think you should go to the river for that
something about leaves and wet silver wind
the howling of the sands
crushed pink and green and silver lights
teeth cutting
strangling fingers that whiten at the bone
no that is wrong
do not ask about them

burn the birch fires

take the highway
past the cattle yards spreading
dark stench to the very edge
wherever you are keep trees in your mind
even if they have fallen and rot
trees that you can pretend are birches

I spend all my days and nights with River now.
In the mornings, we walk outside. We don't take
my bike in case any of the boys see us.

We stop to get a little food in exchange for
whatever flowers I can manage. Usually some
hard bread, maybe a bean pudding.

Then we go to the Library and we read for
hours. Sometimes we lose track of time, sitting
in the stacks holding the books, breathing dust. I
found some large ancient art books with color

pictures of flowers, fields, faces. In one book, the paint swirls and stirs with the spirits of the subjects, the flowers like comets about to explode—what I imagine the fireworks are like in Elysia. Once I found River crying over a picture of blue irises that were beautiful but somehow tormented-looking and another of sunflowers like cyclones; he pretended he wasn't.

At night I sing to River in the cold glass building. Sometimes he joins me, whistling in his high strange way. He is a sweet boy. I would like to fill this place with wonderful blooms, tall as trees, but for some reason all I can produce are famished-looking weeds and thorny brambles. But River wakes each morning and thanks me for them as if they were hundred-petalled peonies.

One night I had a dream. It was about Paul. He took my hand and then we were flying. I saw a city shining below me like the stars in the Desert but much more beautiful. The night was blue-dark and cold, but Paul's hand was so warm that it heated my whole body. I kept trying to see if he had wings, but I couldn't turn my head to him and the lights of the city blinded me. Suddenly we landed in a pink marble room with many walls and alcoves in each wall. People were making love in the alcoves. Paul took me into an alcove and squeezed my body against his. That was all—we just held each other, pressing together through our clothes. But it brought every one of my cells to life.

And it brought back the memory of why I left my home. I still want what I cannot touch.

I woke up and saw River huddled in a corner making stifled gasping sounds. My eyes adjusted to the dark, and it looked like he was plucking something out of his head.

I never said a word. I lay there pretending to sleep until he closed his eyes.

I could not sleep. In the morning, I saw the red marks on River's scalp. Was he pulling his hair out as it grew in?

The next day on our way to the library we heard shouts and River dragged me into the shelter of an abandoned building. Some boys came running through the streets carrying the straw figure of a man covered with feathers. Attached to its neck was what looked like a clear sack full of blood. I recognized a few of the boys from the day I arrived. I felt River's body shivering beside me in the darkness.

The boys drove their sticks into the straw man. Red from the blood sack splattered everywhere.

"What are they doing?" I whispered.

River wouldn't answer. Even when they were gone he didn't want to leave the building. I had to hold his hand all day.

When we got home I asked him again.

"They were killing the demon," he said. "The blood is in a bladder. The demon has feathers."

He looked afraid.

I watched him again that night after he thought I was asleep. He was putting whatever it was he pulled out of his head into a cracked flowerpot. Something about the pained pinched expression of his face and the determination in his eyes reminded me of myself. If there were flowers growing out of my body—and sometimes it seemed that way—I would have ripped them out, too. Self-mutilation is better than any other kind.

When the gray light fell through the glass panes, I noticed a slight blue glow coming from the pot—a reminder of morning in the Desert—and when I looked inside I found a heap of tiny blue feathers hidden there.

"What are these?" I asked him.

He looked ashamed and shrugged.

"River, do you ever do anything that hurts yourself?"

Another shrug.

"I'm not your mother and I can't tell you what to do, but I don't want you to hurt."

He bit his lower lip and his hands went up to his bald scalp.

"It's all right, little one. They are beautiful feathers."

"It's not all right." He started to cry.

67

"Why not?"

"They'll come take me away if they knew I had feathers. Like a devil. I'd rather have them laugh at me bald. They'd give me to the man."

"What man?"

"A man came once and took my Mama away. They say he killed her. That he kills the ones who aren't all human."

I held him in my arms for the first time then. He was so tiny. I felt his heart beating fast against me, the cool of his bare head, the heat of his tears. I thought, this is what it would be like to have a child, to love a child so much that you are no longer just you. Every pain they feel is yours. Different from my love of Paul. Perhaps my love of Paul has to do with not wanting this—this love that is so strong.

River whispered, "I wasn't even born like regular. I was hatched. From an egg."

"An egg? Your mama was a bird?"

"She was part bird. But she was beautiful, really. She was."

"I'm sure she was, River. How could she not be? You are beautiful. And your blue feathers."

"I save them. They remind me of her."

I had heard of the bird-women. I'd never seen one, though. The idea of them frightened me a little—so much of the animal. But suddenly I imagined River hatching from a huge pale blue egg and a sad-eyed woman holding him against her feathered breast.

Tonight I sing to River again, wanting to comfort him, wishing I could bring his mother back. He whimpers in his sleep. I feel my eyes fill with unexpected tears.

And then something happens. I sense it first as a beat of pain in the veins behind my knees and in my neck. Then it is as if the blood is being drained from my body, a sloughing off of my body, pouring out of me in song. And all around the air becomes electric, full of live nerves. Something is coming to life.

Out of the beds of dirt and sand filling the glass building grow plants with thick emerald-green stalks and huge leaves tapering to delicate points. Buds quiver and giant purplish-pink lilies unfold, filling the air with their warm fragrant breath, stretching their stamens out like kisses. River stirs, tucked up there in the empty flower bed, and a smile flickers across his face. Perhaps he has felt the roots spread so suddenly in the dirt beneath him or smelled the perfume in his sleep, felt a gentle dusting of golden pollen. He opens his moist blue eyes and rubs them with his hands.

"Fairy?" he whispers.

"Yes, River."

"What . . ."

He looks around. The lilies tower above him, climbing ever taller toward the dome of the glass palace. He begins to dance around on bare pale feet, the smallest feet, circling the flowers, gazing up at them. He takes my hands and tugs at me. I dance, too, still singing softly.

River joins my song, first whistling, then making up words of his own.

> *Flowers should live.*
> *Mamas shouldn't die.*
> *Houses shouldn't break down.*
> *They shouldn't have fires.*
> *People shouldn't get gardens all messed up,*
>   *or get flowers hurt.*
> *Trees that fall down and everything is just*
>   *in this one heart.*

And more lilies keep growing until we are silent with the dawn.

Down by the water in the still-darkness of morning I hide in the shadows of a tunnel, scanning the shore for a boat that can take me across. They are all chained to their posts, bobbing on the greasy waves. I see a group of boys running down to their vessel, yelling and whistling, their bare feet caked with dirt. I adjust my helmet more tightly over my face and stay in the shadows. If I go to them, they will want me to stay and sing in this Neverland forever. But who else could take me where I want to go? Hardly anyone seems to leave this place.

The boys leap into their boat. I watch them start to sail out into the murk. Maybe I should try to steal one of the other barges. But they all look about to collapse. It seems impossible that the boys' boat is making it across at all.

I reach up, lift my helmet back and touch my head. It feels small and exposed. Last night I wove my hair into one long braid and cut it off. I was going to throw it away, but River wanted to keep it so I let him. In exchange he gave me a necklace made of his blue feathers.

The boys start yelling louder now and pointing. They are yelling, "Giants! Giants! Meat!"

Something in me quivers.

I see a heavy barge emerging from the fog, crossing the water toward me. On the deck I can make out silhouettes of things huge and misshapen.

I remember my childhood dreams and the rocks in the desert. The numbness comes; I can feel my blood stagnate in my veins. My hands become heavy dangling appendages.

"Giants," shout the boys.

The big boat comes closer and I see them better. Giant men with slack jaws and dead eyes. I inhale a stench, even over the smell of toxic water. Something I have smelled recently. The cattle yard along the desert road.

The giants moor their boat and lumber to shore. They carry bloody carcasses of cows thrown over their backs. The dangling, red, veiny bodies look tiny next to the giants. One man could devour a whole animal at one sitting.

I will not be sick. I will not.

I watch the giants chain up their boat and parade into the city, trailing the dead cattle.

I think of how River looked standing there in the thicket of lily blossoms and leaves as I rode away. He had hooked his thumbs through holes in his sweater and they were folded under as if he were trying to keep from putting them in his mouth. I wanted to stop and turn around, lift him in my arms, sit him on my bike, take him with me. He had asked to go, whispering, "I'll be really quiet, Fairy. I don't eat much."

Maybe I should go back to him. Come up with a plan of how to leave. It shouldn't be too hard. And he is so small.

But if I am quick I can jump onto this boat, hide and be carried across. I cannot endanger River this way. I must act quickly. I knead my fingers, trying to make the blood come back. It pricks the nerves.

For a moment I think: Paul. The dream in which we are flying and land in the marble palace. And then I think: Elysia. Even the name is beautiful. I suddenly want to be there more than anything. I try to lose sight of Paul's face. There are only the pink marble alcoves. Yes. Just across that water they are there. The beauty that will help me to forget everything else.

Beauty. I will hypnotize myself with dreams of it as I take my bike down to the water and slip unnoticed and breathing through my mouth onto the foul-smelling ship. And hide down below in a room of blood and ice.

CATTLE YARD

They found me. They say they will make me work on the farm killing cows. They think I am a boy. If they knew that I am a woman they would do worse.

They found me hiding down below before we arrived across the water. The one who saw me first, the one with the slice of scar across his cheek, said he smelled me.

"Fee Fi Fo Fum." And they all laughed and belched. This is the first time in my life I have known terror.

I tell myself over and over, this is a dream. You will wake up in Elysia. The beauty of Elysia stunned you so much that you fell into this nightmare of guilt. You are just guilty because you left River and because your family does not know where you are.

They have locked me into a shack that smells like death. It is dark. They gave me a cow's-skull bowl full of red meat, but I will not eat it. I wonder if they can smell my fear and the ripped sensation in my chest the way they can smell my blood.

The giants come to the one barred window of the shack and bend down to stare in at me. Their eyeballs are shot with red veins and I can smell their breath through the bars.

"Humpty Dumpty sat on a wall Humpty Dumpty had a great fall," growls one of them.

Another retches, "Jack and Jill went up the hill to fetch a pail of water Jack fell down and broke his crown and Jill came tumbling after."

These make them laugh. Their laughter is hot and thick.

"Little boy inside the shack we will not break your back kill a cow and plough a field and we will keep you safely sealed."

I try to sing to myself to keep them away. But my head is stuffed full of their rhymes and there is no music.

"Peter Peter Pumpkin Eater had a wife and couldn't keep her put her in a pumpkin shell and there he kept her very well."

Today Peter Peter has come to bring me the food I won't eat. I am crouched in the corner, staring with burning eyeballs at yesterday's meat buzzing with flies. Last night blood came between my legs. I tried to clean myself as best I could, but I didn't let myself sleep in case I would stain the cot. In my sleep I heard their voices regurgitating the rhymes.

"Little Boy Blue come blow your horn the sheep's in the meadow the cow's in the corn but where is the boy who looks after the sheep? He's under the haycock fast asleep."

The giant has to stoop to enter now, hunching the lump of his shoulders. He puts down the new platter of cow, takes the old meat in his fat-padded fingers and holds it up to my mouth. "Jack Sprat could eat no fat his wife could eat no lean and so between the two of them they licked the platter clean."

I seal my mouth and turn my head away, but he smacks the flesh against my lips. "Could eat no fat could eat no lean."

Suddenly he drops the meat and sniffs the air with his cavernous nostrils.

"Georgie Peorgie Pudding Pie kissed the girls and made them cry." He sniffs again. "Kissed the girls girls girls."

I back away into the corner. His cow-like tongue licks his lips.

"Fee Fi Fo Fum I smell the blood of a woman!"

He rubs his crotch, cupping whatever monstrosity.

"Haycock!"

I feel the fear in the roots of my hair.

I back into the corner. The giant comes closer. His hair is greasy. He reaches out one vast hand.

"Mary Mary quite contrary how does your garden grow? With silver bells and cockle shells and . . ."

The rhymes go on and on. The giant reaches between my legs where I have wadded up some ripped pieces of a sheet under my britches. He presses the steaks of his hands against my chest where my breasts are bound. I am afraid my heartbeat will burst the bandage.

Then I hear the voice. Paul's voice.

Sing, it says. Sing.

I can see Paul riding the waves. The ocean as it was before. I lift my face to that secret light.

her body reclines
a palace
walls are beaten pearl of foam
turrets glazed jade waves
ceiling an opal sky
blue stained rose light
surface breaking into points
of silver teal gold
then white
clouds part again

the sun a door of livid gold
I see it
beyond the blue marbled liquid palace of
    waves
down the changing green to cobalt to that
    steely
gray blue marble of the corridors
cool walls
move liquid lazy changing ever
the columns flashing long glass and white
    silver
bowls of abalone
washed pink green glimmer
fragile shimmer wet even to the dry
iridescence from which to drink wine
that is still almost bitter with salt
the door beckons me
I am trying to reach it
but it is always farther off
and these walls change like marble to water
    to light
I cannot find my way
I keep trying
till the door is gone

I am outside her body
on the sand
and there is only her wrist cut bleeding
soon to be bandaged with night

The giant has staggered backward. Saliva globules spill over his lower lip. He falls against the wall as if I had slammed into his gut. I keep singing. I keep singing. I keep singing.

They all fall away like this. First coming after me from the cattle yards, some of their hands still stained with blood, groping at themselves. Then they almost reach me, but I am singing. I can hardly breathe as I run and sing through the death-laden air.

My motorcycle. Cattle surround it. The metal horse head among the flesh heads of cows. I fling myself into the pen and leap onto the seat. I still have the key on a chain around my neck. Yes.

The giant in the pen groans, "Little Miss Muffett sat on a tuffet eating her curds and whey there came a big spider who sat down beside her . . ."

This seems to strengthen him. He lunges at me. "Bye Baby Bunting Father's gone a-hunting gone to fetch a rabbit-skin to wrap the Baby Bunting in."

Sing of the ocean as it once was. Sing of the healing waves. Wake from this dream of surging groins and gaping mouths.

The motorcycle bursts through the slats of the pen. I feel the wood splintering around me. The once silent cattle now moan in unison as they are freed into the desert.

PAUL

I was the same as you are, Spring. I was haunted by Rafe. He was all I thought about—all I wanted. I thought I could free myself by hating him. Then I thought it would be all right if he went away. Neither of these things worked. Finally I left Elysia with Calliope and Dionisio and you and went into the Desert in search of him. I gave up all the beauty of Elysia to see his face again.

I remember seeing him standing on the other side of the empty ravine. He looked dirty and thin and he was pounding on his drum. He was such a young boy then.

When the water came rushing into the ravine it was like my love for him. When the sands turned to fertile soil, yielding fruit trees and flowers, it was like my joy in him—as if that beauty, that life, were the child he and I could never have.

Now I know that much of that magical life came not from me or Rafe, not from Calliope or Dionisio, not from our music, our band—Ecstasia—but from you, Primavera. Enchanted child. You were the final and essential ingredient in the potion.

I was just like you. I know what it is like to burn for someone. Of course, I cannot tell you this and comfort you the way I have always been

79

able to comfort you since you were born. Because I cannot return your love the way, finally, Rafe returned mine in the musical garden of our creation.

So I understand why you have left us.

But we are mourning, Primavera.

Your mother is unable to play her music. She staggers around like an old, old woman. She is folding in on herself like the flowers that you sang into life and cannot live without you.

Your father paces; he is never still. He grows thin.

Rafe and I stay up all night, unable to warm ourselves. He says to me, "She loves you, doesn't she?"

I tell him the way it was for me before he returned my love. How I would have done almost anything to escape that pain.

He says, "We need her to come back."

We need you back.

RAFE

Did we ever have power to make the earth bloom? I thought I was the river, Paul the sunshine, Calliope the rainbow vision in the air, Dionisio the fertile ground. Ecstasia was why the Desert came alive. I was proud and stupid to think that.

Nothing happened until Primavera sang. And now, will we go back to the way it was before?

The water in the Sound is diminishing to a trickle, the sand sucking it up. I can see the leaves on the trees turning dark and crisp like scabs. The skeleton shapes of the rocks are beginning to show through as their flesh of foliage dies and falls away.

Calliope won't touch her keyboards. Dionisio has stopped laughing. Paul and I don't even hold each other now. Our bed is cold for the first time in all these years.

I try to play my drums, but my hands feel gnarled with age. There is no longer a rhythm inside my body, as if all the blood-rivers there have dried up, too, the islands of organs turned to stone.

I cut my hands on the hard earth, trying to plant, and I weep, but my tears evaporate in the cold dry air even before they touch the ground.

At night I lie beside Paul and I want to touch him but I don't. I try to remember how his sinewy white-hot body feels, a crystalline sword melting to pure light. I have almost forgotten what the torch of his voice sounds like when he sings.

I thought I was some big hero. Maybe I thought I was magical. Now I feel weak, impotent.

Paulo, are we ever going to make love again?

Primavera, will you ever sing for us? I am afraid for you and I am afraid of you, too. All our lives dependent on your songs.

DIONISIO

I'm scared that Calliope is sinking down. One time before she acted this way. But that wasn't even Calliope. That was a long time ago before Primavera was born, when the man from underground sent an imposter Calliope to us—a demon's machine—so that he could keep our Callie for himself. I knew something was very wrong, but I didn't see the difference until the real Calliope returned. I can be an ash-brain sometimes.

This Calliope is the real one, but she has the glazed-over eyes of the creature-Calliope and the grating metal-on-metal voice and the cold hands that won't touch the keyboards. She won't eat anything. All she says over and over is, "Primavera. Primavera. We named her Spring."

"Callie, let's play some music."

But she just shakes her head. She says she can see the flowers dying in front of her eyes. "They wither so much faster than they bloom."

I want to tell our daughter that I love her. She doesn't know. Why didn't I tell her? It was hard to tell the woman she had become. Different than telling the almost boyish, always laughing kid. Maybe if I had told her, she wouldn't have needed to go away. Though I think a lot of it doesn't have to do with me at all. Calliope says a lot of it's Paul. I saw how Primavera looked at Paul, even though I couldn't read her mind like Callie; I pretended I had no idea.

I was lucky that Calliope returned my love. I would have probably suffocated in my own desire if she hadn't. I don't like to imagine our daughter having those feelings for anyone, but of course she would. Look at her parents. Our love for each other has always been like a potent wine. It's like drinking the blood of a god. You never want to stop.

Primavera knew she had to stop—she couldn't even really start. She had to get away from Paul. And from her mother, who could read her thoughts. From her mother's brother, who was also her rival. From her silly thickened father without any powers left to charm her.

CALLIOPE

"I can't see! Let me see!"

I am howling. I am a desert wind, scorching with cold. Dionisio wakes and holds me against his chest. My chill seeps into him and we both shiver.

"Baby-girl. What is it?"

"Primavera!"

"A vision?"

"No. No vision. A feeling. But I can't see! I can't see!"

"What do you feel?"

"Cold. Danger. Pain. Numb. My limbs are numb. Blood. Bleeding. Revulsion."

"Try to see, Calliope."

"She won't let me in. She won't let me see. She can't. She is alone."

"We'll go look for her, Calliope. If you just try to see something to let us know where she is."

"I can't see."

"She's probably in Elysia. We can all go there."

"Without her there is nothing. This whole place we live is a mirage without her. The flowers are dying. Nothing new grows."

My mind has begun to wander away from paradise, into the desert. But I do not find any visions of my daughter there. Only the sand dunes going on forever, the carcasses of dreams, fossils of songs, the picked bones of love.

3. ELYSIA

ARCADIE

The girl and I look alike. We both have thin angular faces and dark hair—though hers is short. We're both tall and thin. She's taller; she's more beautiful. I look sickly and she's all health like she was raised on sunshine and honey. But even so we look like we could be sisters.

She's up there singing on the stage again tonight. I saw her last night when I walked by Moonshine and there she was in the window lit up like a glass of champagne in her short gold tunic. She looks like a beautiful boy. I stood and pressed my face to the glass to see her. I had to keep wiping away the mist of my breath. First thing I saw was how exquisite she was. Then I heard her voice. Singing. It was up there. It was the most most wonderful thing I've heard. But you know it's strange because it made me even colder as I stood out there in the frosty night, on the pavement slicked with ice. It made my heart feel grainy and shrunken. I thought, she is singing for the wrong reasons. I don't know why I thought that. She looked up then, and seemed to look right through the window with her big dark eyes. Maybe she saw me peering in at her. If anyone was ice it was me. She was streaming golden lights and I was just this skinny shivering thing with my face against the glass. She was the magician. The audience sighed and applauded like they were high. Big paper flowers kept falling from the ceiling, opening like fans, and while she sang the girl was reaching into a hat and pulling out an endless string of colored glass baubles shaped like flowers too. I turned away.

But tonight I'm back here. I'm inside and I can see her eyes as she makes cold, silk, greenish lilies grow on ladies' hats. She looks like me. And she is almost in as much pain as I am in. Almost.

I think about him when I wake up in the cold mornings in the bed in the room cluttered with lacy pretty things that have never really been mine and will never feel like mine. We never slept in a bed. He slept standing over me mostly and I lay in the sweet-smelling straw. Some nights he would kneel beside me and press his lips to my cheek till morning. He had the most tender lips, especially for someone so strong.

I think of him all day as I walk in circles around the tent picking up candy wrappers and other waste. He ran here, fast as wind, his hooves scattering electric sparks. He was too big for this place, but at least I could be with him here. Riding him in my green and silver-spangled netting. Sweat poured down my thighs. Sometimes he would glance back at me. I put my hands on his chest and felt his nipples harden between the spread of my fingers. We stopped seeing the tent then. We were in a field of huge wildflowers and butterflies, crashing over a stream into the green green shade of a green green glade. Why didn't we escape and find that paradise? We were afraid. He didn't know if his parents were strong enough to join us. And besides, he said, what if we only find dead Desert? It's enough to be here as long as we can be together. My beloved.

Now you are gone. The man has taken you away and maybe something terrible has happened. I dream of you every night. We're running on a shore beside a clear sea. We're like one creature. A horse with a man's head and torso and a woman's head and torso and legs—one great beast. I wish we were. Then the man would have taken me also and whatever he has done to you would be done to me, too.

PRIMAVERA IN ELYSIA

This city is just like they told me it would be. The air is no different from Neverland, with the same frost and drizzle. The streets are not heaped with trash and sleeping bodies like those streets, but they are dark and my heels crunch into sheaths of gray ice. It is the bars and restaurants that make this a magic place. They flame like the brightest everlasting torches. Huge china dolls with pale iced eyes serve elaborate pastel pastries and many-faceted crystal goblets of perfumed drinks. Balloons float as if borne up by the layers of music, and people in gorgeous costumes of feathers and glinting beads dance dreamily, blowing soap bubbles.

Mirrors are everywhere. I have seen my portrait, my reflection in the fragments of my mother's tiny broken pocket mirror, in the lake and in the lenses worn by the man, Gunn, but I have never seen a full, clear, real image of Primavera. I take off the helmet and touch my cropped hair. My own eyes startle me. They look colder than I feel.

I find a place called Lunatic. The figures seem to hover over the polished floor, shadowless and shimmering like images in a dream. There are women in gowns of voluminous taffeta or embroidered satin, waving lacquered fans, clowns with powdered faces and multicolored jingling costumes, people with veils trailing from high-peaked hats. Elegant chilly music vibrates and the crowd dances languidly. Sweet smoke from their cigarettes clouds the air and light plays on the fluted champagne glasses in their hands.

Their eyeballs slide over me. I shiver as a woman in white velvet drifts by with a man at each arm. My fingers feel as if they have rubbed the velvet pile backwards. I can smell the woman's strong perfume. It is deep and poisonous. The woman laughs and flings back her head so that her throat gleams bare, pale as her dress. The men laugh with her and whisper in her jewelled ears.

The music changes to a kind of minuet and a couple in powdered wigs and pale blue taffeta begin a precise dance—pointing their rosette-adorned slippers, gazing, bowing. Others join in, kaleidoscoping slowly around the room with expressions enamelled onto their faces.

I sit by myself. Men dressed as emperors, clowns, and pirates with swords pass me without a glance from their shadowed eyes or a twitch of their lips. Another shiver goes through me.

A man with a black snake painted on his cheek and a stuffed parrot on his shoulder approaches. I smile, but he does not respond and walks away. Turning, I see a white-skinned woman in a black leather corset stretch out a gloved hand to him; they move onto the dance floor. The woman bares large white teeth between her crimson lips.

I stare into the flashing fusion of crystal and light, the hypnotic motion of the dancers. The high notes of music are like fingers on the keys of my nerves. I feel blinded, confused.

Suddenly the music stops. The clown with the snake and parrot points at me and shouts, "What are you doing here?" They all join him. The room grows dark and then someone shines a circle of light on me.

I stand up with platelets of cold rising on my bare arms. The people stare at me from behind fans with cut-out holes for their eyes, from behind satin half-masks. They lick their lips. I sing.

> *wander the gallery*
> *white partitions*
> *and find us everywhere*
> *bodies projected*
> *like ghosts*
> *in a haunted house*
>
> *an aquarium filled with*
> *skulls and conch shells*

electric green water
where we writhe and tumble

or I am lying
down on the table
in glitter tutus
the fake blood ready
you start to sever
with huge steel blades
then stop and climb up
thrust back releasing
magic birds

or I am painting
huge pink lilies
you come up placing
against my hipbones
tentative fingers

the last exhibit is the bed
your wrists are white and broad

like altars

My voice sounds weak and off-key. I think, maybe they will attack me or at least throw me out. Or maybe just laugh, which would perhaps be the most terrifying thing I could imagine, having heard the one demon laugh of the woman in white.

I want there to be flowers, but I knew there will not be. They could not grow in this place.

All the flowers here are paper, silk, lace, or jew-elled. What I used to want.

And I get what I had wanted, what they want. The flowers that blossom suddenly on their gowns and in their lapels are gaudy, stiff—and lifeless. The ones that shower from the high ceil-ing are the very same.

They love it. They applaud and howl. I sing with more strength.

This is what I once wanted.

Night after night I sing for them and they swoon, they cry out. Is it because they are en-chanted by my voice, or do they just love the pretty things I make for them? They fight over the rhinestone configurations that do not even look like any real flower I have ever seen. What has happened to my real flowers?

I remember River. Asleep and holding the braid of my hair against his chest. How could I take care of him while I tried to find success in Elysia? I asked myself when I left.

How could I have left him? I ask myself now.

I no longer wear his feather necklace. The stones I sing and wear at my throat never get warm.

Tonight I am at a bar called Moonshine, and I feel bloodless and trembling as I stand on the stage trying to make the crowd love me.

All I can think of is sitting in the special garden in the shade of real flowers, singing for Paul. And River. I think of River alone.

I look up and see the girl standing at the back of the room. She wears a long white cloak and her hair is wet. It streams down her shoulders. Her eyes are very sad. I feel that I know her, that she is someone close to me, although I have never seen her before in my life.

Maybe it is just that she is in pain the way I am in pain.

Or perhaps in more pain.

At the end of my show I go over to her.

"You sing beautifully," she says.

"Thank you."

"You're not from here."

"No."

"I could tell. Do you like it here?"

"Yes. It's what I wanted." I hope I do not sound as if I am trying to convince myself.

She looks at me carefully and I feel the same way I do when my mother reads my thoughts. In fact, she has eyes like my mother's—slightly slanted, dark and wise.

"Where are you staying?" she asks.

"I have a room in a hotel around the block."

It is a powder-blue room with a quilted blue satin bed, pink cherubs and wreaths of roses painted on the walls. It is always cold there. I pay for it with jewel-encrusted songs. Sometimes I feel like the cherubs are small blood-suckers, demanding the life in my veins for a night's rest. Suddenly I think of the giants and my hands go numb. I rub the palms together.

"Do you want to stay with me?" asks the girl.

I don't even know her. What is she offering me this?

"If you change your mind," she says, "my name is Arcadie." She hands me a tiny card and turns away.

I watch her walk out into the rain.

I sit alone on the satin bed staring at my re-flection in a mirror. I am still wearing my makeup and I hardly recognize the powdery girl in the glass with her gleaming red lips. She looks like the drifting white-velvet woman with the de-monic laugh from Lunatic. I try to see deep into her eyes to find her soul. Sugary-looking cherubs hover over her head, pointing fat fingers at her as if to say, you left that little boy all alone, you left your family, your mother is weeping. The mirror-girl's soul is deeply buried or gone altogether.

The young girl, Arcadie, haunts me. I think of her face as I try to warm myself under the per-petually chilly satin sheets. Why is she so famil-iar? I wish I had gone with her. Even dripping rainwater she had a warmth about her that none of the others had. I think of the white horse that I saw in the field at home the morning I left. There is something about Arcadie's large brown eyes and her narrow pale limbs and the mane of hair that reminds me of that horse.

Paul is also like a horse with his long stride, his powerful neck. I wish he was here. We could sing together on the stage in the spotlight. But Paul would say, "I'm too old, Primavera, I can't go back there." Would he even admire me with my ice-cold flowers and my red lips? Or would he turn away, shaking his head.

I push the silver tray of pastries across the marble table. Miniature turrets of cake and cream, swirls and puffs and rolls and tarts. The sugar has made my teeth ache and my pulse quicken. I try to remember why I came here at all.

calla lilies are almost green they're so white
  she said
and if I had a party I'd encase them in ice

she painted flowers on her cheek and he
  sang

then they went out into the night
to lie on some stars on the boulevard
to stand in the fountain

into a white garden of lace
and he sang about a mirage she had seen
where leopards wandered and green birds

he moved as if someone was lurching his
    strings and she thought
for a moment when she saw his body slump
    into the light
with his white mask and his blue eyes and
    his urgent voice contracting
expanding
she thought that
yes
she wanted him
or what was this

but she was only a doll
but she crumpled anyway
the white tulle of her dress forming a flower
into which she sank down with her gauze
    hair
her large porcelain hands and her frail
    lidded eyes
he kept right on singing
about stars that had fallen out of the sky
    onto the street
he kept singing fingering a piece of white
    tulle
maybe he knew what had happened
maybe he thought only
of the leopards and the green white lily
    birds dancing through an ice jungle
he could not taste the salt of her sweat on
    his lips anymore

he closed his eyes
the scars on his face had begun to show

through the layers and layers of white paint

Through the glint and gleam of my song I see the faces of the audience as if they are very far away. Veils, fans, feather headdresses, hats like canopies.

I feel as if someone put a syringe into me and is sucking out little drops and putting them into all the things everywhere. My eyes caught in a pair of rhinestone earrings, my heart-blood in that sparkling pink brooch. And I am left a bone puppet.

The man who sits in the back of the bar is someone I've seen before. Lipless mouth. Metal man. He is wearing me in his eyes. Two Primaveras captured in glass. I remember the way I used to see myself in my father's gentle eyes. I danced there.

Now my throat constricts as if scraped with cut glass shards.

I see an image of my motorcycle with the horse's head rearing up, sparks flying, sounds skidding from the metal mouth.

Gunn is the name I remember. Gunn.

Metal tang shocking my teeth.

I stop singing and run backstage.

Arcadie is standing in the wings.

"It's just that I feel a strange connection to you," she says. "When I first heard you singing, I thought I had found a sister I had lost."

I nod, unable to speak.

"Come stay with me," she whispers.

I look into her eyes and see my mother's tenderness, a kind of depth, a giving of the self. Sometimes in my mother it terrified me, but now I yearn for that.

There is a place in the Desert where huge date palms surround a rainbow pool and the water jewels the throats of the tree trunks with tremulous shadows. Swans swim there, bluebottles skim. Huge flowers clamber up the trunks of the palms and spill down the bank. The air sparkles with the pale sheen of many colors.

It was my mother's favorite place. When I was a child, she and I would go there and watch the swans. She called it the Swannery. I felt safe. But as I grew older I didn't like it anymore. I couldn't breathe there.

With Arcadie I remember how the Swannery used to feel. It was protected and sweet. It was a place of women where men were not needed, where everything was lush, nothing dry, rigid.

I follow Arcadie out of the bar without even gathering any of the rhinestone and filigree butterflies that cover the floor.

Outside it is still raining. It hardly ever stops. I put on my helmet, but she lets the drizzle fall on her bare head. She is smaller than I am and I feel a desire to use my coat to cover both of us.

We get on my motorcycle and I take her hands, place them on my hips. We pass a green neon mermaid flashing and I think of the dead mermaid I saw by the sea. This one will never die. She has green neon nipples winking on and off and a mean mouth.

Arcadie's apartment is up some stairs. We enter the small room cluttered with objects. Everywhere lace, dolls, fans, perfume bottles, masks, vases, shoes, ribbons.

"These things aren't really mine," she says, almost apologizing. "There was someone who lived here before."

I nod. I have never seen anything like this. I touch a pale peach satin slipper festooned with bows. A china doll with startling glass eyes and long blond braids bares tiny pearled teeth. Frosted glass bottles and enamelled boxes cover the surface of a dressing table. Who lived here before Arcadie? Who owned these wreaths and beads and baubles?

All over the walls there are pictures of a young girl, a man, and a woman. The girl's face is small and her chin comes to a sharp point. Her eyes are sunken into bluish shadows. In one picture she wears a frilled costume and a small crown of jewels on her head. The man and woman embrace her so tightly that none of them seem free to move separately.

"Would you like to eat?" Arcadie asks me.

Suddenly I am aware of the hunger I have been feeling. It seems to permeate my bones.

I sink into pink cushions while Arcadie goes to the kitchen. She brings me a bowl of hot soup and a small loaf of bread. The food reminds me of my mother's meals; it's not like the cakes and ices I have been living on since I arrived here.

"Who is the girl in the pictures?" I ask.

"Why?"

"I don't know. There is something about her."

Arcadie nods. "Yes. Her name was Liliastrom."

She reaches for a tattered book bound in leather. She opens it carefully, turning the pages, looking for something, and I glimpse the frail tracery of lettering.

"Here," she says.

While I read she leaves the room.

THE DIARY

He hurt me tonight. He hurt me so much and I will still go back to him. I need my fix. But I hurt all inside.

And this is the time of the month when the egg slips down. What if he caught it?

Who will be born? What will a child of his be?

Mother and Father. Why aren't you here? I need you now. I've done this all for you but look at me! And I'm still going to go back. I'm going to go back to him. I can't stop. Help me stop. Someone.

When I take this drug you're right here. It's like you never died. I can even touch you. He is a great and terrible master that he can make a drug that brings back the dead.

He took me into his train. He lives inside a broken train and he took me there and threw me against the wall and pulled up my dress and stuck his body into me. His breath smells like rot. I hate him. I want to scrape my insides clean. I can't stop going down to him.

Who is he? They say he's just a man who came from the Desert with his family and then grew old and went Under and changed. He used to be a healer, they said. And then he started making these drugs. The magical Orpheus that brings back the dead is the only one I need.

Now the way I feel I may need it to bring me back. Does that make any sense? Will anyone ever try to bring me back from the dead with Orpheus? What will it make me feel like? What do you feel Mother, Father? You tell me with your eyes you want me to keep bringing you back.

I hate the man who gives me my Orpheus but how I love Orpheus. He is worth any-thing—beautiful killing god of resurrection. Even this.

Arcadie comes back in. Her hair is pulled away from her face and her skin has an almost eerie radiance.

"I don't understand," I say, handing the journal back to her.

She opens it to another page.

Strange how a baby makes you love it right away. Even a baby whose father almost murdered you when he broke into your body. I want to get rid of this child, whisper to the spirit hovering near me looking for a home, go away, come again later, I can't have you now. But already I feel the suckling sweetness inside of me and I cannot let go.

I am so thin that no one will probably know for a long time. I can wear clothes that disguise it. Toward the end I will take time away from the circus. When the baby is born I will take it down below and hide it. What else can I do?

Oh, why did you choose me? Why did you choose now? Your father is Death and your mother is an Addict and you are fated to be born under the earth in a land of phantoms.

Maybe someday you will return to the light. If you ever find this book, know that I loved you enough to hold onto you. I had to give you up. Give you down.

"I still don't know what this means, Arcadie."

"I'll tell you," she says. She looks into the mirror and touches her cheek. Then she looks back at me.

"I never knew my parents. I was raised underground in the sewer city. I lived in a home full of old people with withered skin and broken hearts. You could see that their hearts were broken by looking into their eyes. For the longest time I thought everyone had broken hearts and was ancient looking. Even the others, the Addicts I saw on the streets sometimes, had skin like peeling ash. They howled in the night as if pieces of them were being cut off.

"Don't think I grew up in a complete nightmare. The old people loved me and I loved them. Especially Violina. She taught me to read even though books were almost nonexistent down there. Reading and writing saved me, I think. I would have died Under otherwise.

"When I was a little older, I saw some young people from Elysia wandering around underground. They looked like visions. Exquisite. I ran away, afraid they would hate me.

"I told Violina about it. She gave me a key and a map. She said that the time had come; there was a place I could go to aboveground. But I never thought of leaving. I was a little under-child, always cold and aching. I thought that everyone had night sweats and ache-bolts in their heads. The old people talked to me. They told me of their youth above. It was like a dream—not a real place I could ever go to. I never really wanted to go there. Why live some-where where you'd just end up being hated when you aged? I thought that everyone ended up down below anyway, so why be laughed at by those pretty ones? I thought of myself as a little old thing, too. Shrunken.

"Then finally I got to see what I had missed. Can you imagine what Elysia looks like to a child who has never known anything but stale air, dark streets, bent bodies, bleak empty corridors full of death? Heaven is what it looked like. It's not."

"How did you finally come here, then?" I ask.

"Violina died. I was used to death by then— Old Ones were always dying. But it was different with Violina. She had been very kind to me. I wanted to die, too. I drifted around under-ground, pretending I was dead.

"Then the hero and his friends came to tell all the Old Ones they could leave if they wanted.

The hero was going to lead them to paradise, he said, a place where they could live in peace, not chastised, not segregated. The man was lean, dark, and beautiful. Do you know what? I pretended he was my father. It was my secret game. I had never known my father, and this man was the right age and even had the same lean angled bones. I was too afraid to talk to him, though. I wondered if maybe he was a god of some sort. There were rumors that he and his friends had made a paradise in the Desert just by playing music."

I feel my breath catch and rip as if there are nails in my throat. She goes on.

"Music! I'd never heard any. He played a small drum. It made me weep. He was playing my blood rhythms. I imagined what I would say to him. I'm really your daughter; take me back with you. But always so afraid. I did follow him up though, like a person sleepwalking, half blind with my tears, in line with the Old Ones who had also chosen to leave. I noticed how tall and straight he stood. Everyone I knew walked with the weight of down below. I vowed to walk like the hero, Rafe Dunes."

Rafe Dunes.

"And I would have followed him back across the Desert to a place where flowers grew and rivers ran, but what did that mean to me when I had seen Elysia? City of sparklers and rum, candy swans and gilt. I reeled through the streets, forgetting that they might laugh at me— an under-child. The people all looked like gods and goddesses. I forgot about the hero leading the Old Ones away to his paradise. I was still young. This city could be mine. And then I saw the circus and there was never another question in my mind that I was home.

"He cantered around the ring. He was a man and at the same time a horse. He looked into my eyes and there was a quaking in my chest.

"We were an act. I'd dress up in frothy skirts and climb up onto his horse-back. The white fur was sleek but bristled against my thighs. I wanted to touch his man-back, which was broad and lithe, different from his lower body, more familiar to me and yet so mysterious as well. I'd never seen a young man unclothed, much less a horse-man. He smelled always like meadows, what I imagine meadows are like, although I'd never been in one.

"For a long time we didn't talk. I think I might not even have been sure that he spoke the same language. We told each other things with our eyes, though, and with our bodies in motion around the ring.

"Then one night during the performance, both of us drenched with sweat, he turned his neck and looked at me. 'Let's keep going,' he said.

"I must have seemed startled.

"He said, 'Yes, I speak. We just try to stay quiet around most of you. Shall I keep going?'

"I nodded and he charged through the filmy curtains of the tent, past the drunken crowds and into the night. The air was like a cascade of liquid silver beads. I heard his hooves on the cobblestones. They struck sparks.

"We wanted to ride outside of the city, but we didn't know where to find meadows. There was only the Desert beyond, we had been told. So we raced through the city, past the bars full of cakes and wine, past the Ferris wheel, the carousels with their carved wooden horses that could never leave.

" 'We can't leave either,' he said to me. We'd stopped in the shadows beside an empty carousel still turning through the night. The horses were in a frozen frenzy.

"I buried my face against his neck, touched his man-back at last. It was as warm as his lower body. He turned and arched so I slid off of him. He caught me in his arms and steadied me. We were face-to-face for the first time. His lips were so soft, so soft but with the hard pressure of his teeth underneath.

"In the shadows at the edge of the deserted carousel the horse-man and I caressed and kissed. I felt a healing strength fill my body. He whispered to me, asking who I was, where I'd come from. He told me about the faraway fields where his parents had been born, how they had been captured and brought to Elysia. I told him about Violina. We spoke of the books that we loved, the words that had saved us. He spoke poems he remembered. When the sky was light, he carried me back to the circus. I went inside my tent alone and lay back, exhausted, delirious. I knew then I would never love anyone else. It's strange how the heart knows these things.

"The next day we were silent, pretending we had never spoken. But at night we slipped away again. And soon after that I came to his tent while he slept—standing up, his neck bent, nostrils flared—and I stroked his shoulders until he opened his eyes.

"After that night our love was like a child, so solid and warm and miraculous. We never had a child, though. My beloved was afraid of the horse hooves in my womb, but I wasn't. I would have had his child. I wanted a centaur baby that looked just like its father to come out of me."

Not me, I thought, but I didn't say anything. I was afraid of having any child. But the thought of one with hooves?

"One day the man came and took my lover and his parents away.

"I wandered the streets howling like a demon. I was in too much pain to even wish for my own death. I was a monster of pain. All the wounds he had healed when he touched me opened jagged and raw and new wounds worse than these.

"I came to this place, this apartment. It was on the map Violina had given me. I even had the key. I had never thought of coming here before because all I wanted was the circus. But after the man took my lover away, I found these rooms full of lace and shiny things. I screamed in these rooms every night. I thought the china dolls' eyes would shatter. Later, when I found the journals, I learned that the woman who had lived here before had suffered, too.

"Listen."

She opens another journal and reads.

"My child. Your eyes are dark. To me they are like bruises. Your hair is thick already. I am afraid one day it will strangle you. When I look at you all I can see is Death's rape. I can see a tiny version of his skeleton under your perfect skin. Forgive me.

"I hate myself for not being able to give you love, for not being able to give you a world of warmth, light, beauty. How pale you are, how small, how in need of nourishment.

"And I am pale and small and starving, too.

"All I can give you is away. I can give you to the Old Ones who live below. They will cherish you. They will love you much more than I am able to.

"I can give you a name. I want to give you a name that will become the flowery, peaceful world you should be born into.

"I will call you Arcadie and hope you find that world."

"Who was that woman?"

"My mother. They called her Lily."

"Lily?"

She nods, her heavy hair swaying.

"My mother's brother Rafe knew a woman named Lily."

"Rafe, the hero."

"Yes. Rafe Dunes."

"And your mother's name is Calliope."

"Yes."

"It's in the journal. Lily met Rafe after she gave birth to me. My father was a man named Doctor who lived underground and gave Lily a drug called Orpheus, which made her dead parents return to her in her mind."

Doctor. I shudder, remembering the stories Paul told me of the man with the face like a skull who lived underground and manufactured drugs that quickened a terrible desire, made a demon spring bloom or brought back the dead. Not even Paul told me much, though. I only knew that now Doctor was dead.

"Is it the way I think it is, Primavera?"

"Doctor was my mother's father. And Rafe's."

"Your grandfather and my father were the same man," she says.

Arcadie and I stare at each other. The room is hushed. I think I can almost hear the chattering of the china dolls' tiny teeth.

Arcadie closes her eyes, asleep.

We go into the plaza to see the horses. Arcadie loves horses, although she says has never seen one. Only stone horses. And a man with the lower body of a horse.

She points up at the stone statues with the torches set into their eyes and mouths. The burning eyes and mouths seem painful. I think I can hear the horses screaming.

"The white horse is the symbol of the poet and the artist," she says. "The white horse is the dream symbol of male love and beauty. It is masculine sexual passion and young strong creative inspiration together."

"You think of him always," I say softly.

As if she hasn't heard me: "It is also linked to death," she says.

LILY'S DIARY

Rafe came to me last night. His hair was damp from the rain and smelled like a greenhouse. Wet, like that, he was just the image of the boy in my river dream. I pulled him into the warm room where it was dark.

He said, "I want to see you when we come. Let me light some candles."

I was afraid of those sets of glowing eyes watching us, revealing me to him.

"No. The dark is better."

Age spots have already started to speckle my hands.

I want to push him away. I know that so soon we will no longer have each other. I will be old and horrible because of this drug I take to bring my parents back, and he will still be a young man with smooth unlined skin.

And I want to keep him with me forever in a cage of love. Blindfold him. Stroke his hair and his cheek until I perish.

Why didn't I have Rafe's child instead of that man's? If I had met Rafe before all of this began, we could be together with our child, safe from Under. At least for awhile. It's strange because the baby I had looked like she could have been Rafe's daughter, her eyes so bright with darkness and her delicate bones. Maybe I had Rafe's child although I didn't know it and though our bodies hadn't touched yet. Some miraculous joining of our spirits.

I miss my baby. She'd be older now. Sometimes when I go down I feel this terrible tugging to go and see her, but I'm afraid it wouldn't be fair. I can't bring her back up and take care of her now—it's too late. And something about her frightens me. She reminds me too much of her father and the gutting pain of him.

But I'll be going Under for good very soon. Maybe before I die I can hold her in my arms again. I'll pretend she's Rafe's baby. Maybe I could even tell Rafe about her and he could take care of her. His sister looks so kind; maybe Calliope could raise my daughter aboveground when I'm gone.

Last night when Rafe was inside of me, I thought, this is my real Poet, the true Orpheus. This is the elixir that makes life from death. My parents are gone, but this boy brings me to life and in me Mother and Father are alive.

But it is too late now. I am dying just as my parents died. I want to tell Rafe, "Don't ever try to find me again after I go. Or anyone. Don't try to bring back what is lost."

But deep inside of me is a secret. That I want him to find the Orpheus and give me life as I gave my parents life. So that this love could go on as long as he lives.

No. It would destroy him. I must just love him now and remember his body filling me with a healing, singing river when the Orpheus calls me to him for the final time.

* * *

Lily. Rafe's first love before Paul. Lily who died so soon.

Rafe must have been so beautiful, so young, coming out of the rain to Lily's door that night.

Paul must have suffered when he saw Rafe with Lily. He could never be that small delicate girl in the circus petticoats. He had deep scars on his cheeks and he was a man.

Paul must have felt the way I felt that night on the rocks when I said that I loved him. Caught in the wrong body. Paul understood.

So I need to understand Paul. As much as I want him—his love—as much as I want with him what Rafe and Lily had—here, in this very room of dolls and satin cushions—I need to remember that Paul loves Rafe. They have saved each other's lives. They have held each other through death. They have traveled away from the city of their desire to find each other in a barren desert. And they have made paradise there.

That is what I want. Maybe not Paul, but I want someone to love that much. The way Paul and Rafe love each other, my mother and father, the way Lily and Rafe once loved and Arcadie and her horse-man.

Arcadie, my sister, my mother, my friend.

She cooks for me in the steaming kitchen. There are pale plush towels and lavender soaps in her bath. We dress up in circus costumes and sit on the pink cushions, reading. I comb Arcadie's long hair, smoothing out the tangles. She tells me stories. Arcadie writes her stories down in leather books that look like Lily's journals.

"How did you know about us?" I ask her tonight.

We have taken our baths and our skins glow in the lamplight. Especially hers. She looks like a young child.

"I had heard stories of Rafe's sister who had given birth to a girl who could sing flowers. I heard you sing and I knew. Also I could tell by your eyes. You and I have some darkness in us that comes from that man who lived underground. It is stronger in me because I have more of his blood and because I grew up down there. But it's in you, too."

"I feel as if I'm suffocating sometimes."

"So do I."

"I never understood it. I was always surrounded by light and air and flowers, but somehow I always felt as if I was being buried."

Arcadie closes her eyes. She puts her hand to her chest.

"Are you all right?"

"I get tired."

"Can I bring you something?"

"I'm all right." She leans back and closes her eyes. Her eyelashes brush her cheek and I think of her horse-man.

"Arcadie?"
But she does not respond. She is asleep.

In the morning, I walk into the bathroom and find her staring at her reflection, patting the corners of her eyes.
"What's wrong?" I ask.
She looks at me, startled. Her hand moves quickly, hiding something under the sink. "Nothing."
"You fell asleep so fast last night again."
"It happens sometimes. I need to be by myself now."
I leave her there at her secret ritual.
I sing myself to sleep.

> *the night is glazed with light*
> *petticoats and perfumed necks*
> *horror swept up in yards of glossy lace*
> *beauty she bares her teeth*
> *but her breasts are soft and sweet as wet*
>   *leaves*
> *and she dances white*
> *glistening in the dark*
> *waiting for us*

Terror dreams.
There are people cutting off parts of their faces and bodies bit by bit, nose, ears, eyes, as slowly as possible until they die.

I am being buried alive. I can't breathe. Choked on dirt and worms.

I wake up coughing. I call for Arcadie but she is not in her bed. I look out the window and see a slender figure in white under the street lamplight. I put on my coat over my nightgown, put on my boots and run downstairs, outside.

Arcadie is racing through the streets. I think of calling to her, but I decide I will follow in silence. The night is cold and I can see the frost blossoms of my breath. They remind me of the flowers I once sang.

Some beautiful boys and girls, nursing on huge glass-nippled bottles, dance along. Arcadie dodges away from them. They pass me laughing and I smell the sharp-sweet liqueur on their breath.

Through the winding streets. My chest aches. My bare feet hurt inside my boots. There will be blisters.

Finally Arcadie stops at an opening in the cobblestones. I cannot contain myself.

"Arcadie!"

She turns to me. Her eyes are so sad. I think she is going to run away, but instead she holds out her hand.

"You are going Under?" I say.

"Yes," she whispers, the words becoming flowers that vanish as soon as they appear.

I look down at the opening. I heard how the tunnel to Under beckons to people with melodies, but all it offers me is icy air and descent.

"Will you take me with you?"

"Are you sure you want to?" she asks.

"I've always wondered about it."

"If I was born in the place you were I'd never go searching for Elysia or especially Under."

"But then I wouldn't have found you," I say.

We look at each other.

"No one seems to ever remember what the tunnel is like," she says. "Maybe that's better."

Is she warning me?

We go down.

We are waiting on the shore in the darkness, listening to the eel-like water slithering past. A few cloaked people stand with their heads lowered. One of them turns to me and I see the face with nose and one ear missing like in my dream.

"Abomination," the voice wheezes. "Abomination. Abomination."

I turn and see a light, hear a whistle. The boat approaches.

"Be careful of the water," Arcadie says.

"Why?"

"They say it can make you lose your voice."

I put my hand to my throat.

The boat man glares at us and spits into the river.

"No wonder that water can make you lose your voice," I say. I am trying not to seem afraid.

Arcadie pays the boat man with some coins, which he pops into his mouth.

"He eats metal," she whispers to me.

We go to sit in the back of the boat, carefully avoiding the puddles of water.

"Don't let me sleep," she says. "Please."

"What do you mean?"

"Later on. While we're down here."

"You can't sleep. You are my guide." I look around the boat. "Are they Addicts?" I whisper.

She shrugs.

"But there isn't any Orpheus anymore is there?"

"Not that I know of."

"If someone you loved died and you could get some, would you take it?"

"It killed my mother, but I understand why she took it. The person comes back to you in the flesh like they never left."

"Why do you come here, Arcadie?"

"Please don't ask me."

We arrive at the other side of the shore.

"In a way I wish he were alive," I say as we step off the boat.

"Who?"

"Doctor. I wish I knew what he was like so I could understand myself better."

"I've never wanted to see or even hear about that man. I could hardly read my mother's journals. I don't want to see Death's face."

"Then why do you come down here?"

"Not for Death. I come for beauty."

I look at the subway cars rusting among piles of bones and debris. A few Addicts are sleeping huddled in a forest of weeds just out of reach of the river that can steal your voice. I wonder if the river is full of the voices it has stolen, if they sing and scream together sometimes, if the people who once owned them dance in desperation on the shore with arms outstretched toward the gloating water.

This is the place Arcadia comes for beauty?

She must know what I'm thinking. "You'll see," she says.

We step carefully toward the broken-down subway train.

I have a strange feeling of returning to somewhere I have been before.

Through the cracked window of one car I see a figure. Familiar. When I was very small she looked like this, her dark hair streaming and her face so round and smooth. Holding me. Singing with me. In the Swannery of rainbow waters. I want to run to her. Why did I leave her?

My mother.

I rush up the metal steps and through the door. Arcadie is behind me.

We are not in a grotto of swans and palms. In this cold metal tunnel of the train there are many many dolls covered with cobwebs and dust. Among them stands the woman who looks just like my mother looked many years ago. But something is very wrong with her.

"Don't be afraid," the woman says in a voice like my mother's only not.

"This is Primavera," Arcadie tells her.

The woman nods stiffly. How strange. To see your mother the same age as yourself.

"Who are you?" I ask.

"Doctor made me to look like Calliope. I am not Calliope. I am only a doll. Doctor died. I'll never get old. I will remain down here forever. Under underground."

"Doctor made you?"

"He could make anything. But he never made me really alive. He forgot my heart. Will you stay with me?"

"Arcadie," I say. "What is this? She looks just like my mother."

"I don't know. It must be what she says. Didn't your parents ever tell you about anything like that?"

"They never liked to say what happened down here. How did you find her?"

"I met her when I came down looking for something."

"She was looking for Orpheus," the creature says. "It brings back the dead. I will never die, but I would if I could. There's no more Orpheus, though."

"Why are we here then, Arcadie?"

"Aphrodite. Aphrodite. Aphrodite Oil," says the creature.

She walks off among the rows of dolls with cracked glass eyes and decaying wigs of hair. Arcadie follows her and I follow Arcadie.

The next subway car is lit with a greenish glow. The air is moist and everywhere grow strange plants. The blossoms remind me of huge bleeding mouths gaping at us. I think that one of them snaps at me as I pass. We hurry through, following the thing that looks so much like my mother.

We come to still another car filled with glass jars of weird-looking things. Roots that resemble appendages—or *are* they fingers, toes, and hands? Jars of dirt that seems to move as if infested with tiny living creatures. Jars of bones.

In the next car there are rows of giant vats. The creature stirs one. She is my mother's size but much stronger. The stick she uses is almost as tall as she is, but she moves it easily through the thick potion.

There is a heavy scent in the air. I feel sleepy

and Arcadie looks as if she is about to collapse. But she keeps walking. She is determined.

Finally, in the fifth subway car, the creature pauses. There are shelves covered with tiny, glinting, milky, tear-shaped jars. She takes one down and hands it to Arcadie.

"Now remember, don't use too much," she says.

"Can I please have another?"

"No. No. You mustn't use too much. Too sleepy. You'll come back here when it runs out."

"But it's hard for me to come down here."

"Under underground. Don't lose what you've found. You must come back and visit me. And your friend, too. I get lonely. I can't give you any more now. Not any more," chatters the voice.

"What is it?" I ask, squeezing Arcadie's hand to keep her awake.

"Aphrodite Oil. It makes you stay young and beautiful."

"You are young and beautiful."

"Come on," she says. "Let's go."

"No, no, stay and play. Stay with me. I get so lonely. All alone."

"We can't stay now," Arcadie says.

"But you'll be back. You're like me now. You'll never get old, will you? You'll come back here forever?"

"Yes. We'll be back. Good-bye."

"Good-bye," calls the mechanical voice after

us as I pull Arcadie through the train to the car full of dolls and then outside into Under.

Paul, Rafe, my parents came here when they were young, just my age. They loved bright lights and sweet pretty things. This place must have seemed like hell to them. Maybe this place is hell.

Arcadie and I walk across the dark littered field toward the buildings. "I just need to find a mirror," she keeps saying.

Under reminds me of Elysia—the winding streets and angled walls seem to follow the same plan—but an Elysia without any sparkle: the carcass, the bones. No soul. Does Elysia have a soul? Or is it just a corpse dressed up and strung with lights?

We walk down the street holding hands. A few old people wrapped in yards of pale fabric drift by. Not all of them went with Rafe the hero. Some chose to remain. They turned down paradise. But then, I'm here, too. I did the same thing.

Some bodies lie in the gutter. Sleeping? I hear sobs coming from somewhere.

"Here," Arcadie says.

She pulls me into a building. Over the door is a red neon sign: UNDER.

I can hardly see with all the red smoke. Only the vague outline of figures crouched on tables, tied to the walls or suspended by ropes from the ceiling. I stumble into stone creatures with bulging eyes and phalluses three times the size of their bodies. Loud music blasts us, filling my head with electric currents of pain. If beautiful music can create a paradise, what is this doing?

Arcadie leads me through this maze and into a room in the back. It is tiny and smells of urine. But she doesn't care. There is a mirror here.

She looks into it. Slowly, tenderly, she removes the stopper from the bottle.

"What is it?"

"It really works. It's amazing. The only problem is it makes you sleepy."

"How did you find it?"

"I came down here looking for something to stop the pain when the man took my lover away. Either I wanted to find some of the Orpheus to bring him back if he had died, or I wanted something to make me brave enough to leave Elysia and find him. Or at least a drug that would take away my nightmares—nepenthean. They like that word down here."

I want to hold her. She looks so vulnerable. Her hand shakes as she pours a few drops of the oil onto her palm. It shines, iridescent.

"I read in my mother's diary that Doctor had lived in the subway, that he made his drugs there. So I went and I found that woman-thing all alone wandering around talking to herself. Doctor had left a recipe for the beauty oil and

125

she made it. That's all she did. She was so lonely. She thought she'd be there forever, growing those plants and extracting their essence, mixing it with the other ingredients and brewing the oil. She wanted me to use it so I could be young like her always, so I'd keep coming back."

Arcadie has a wild look in her eyes. Then she closes them, breathes deeply and rubs some of the oil onto her face. It gleams in the reddish light.

"It might not be safe," I say. I am really thinking that I would like to feel the oil slick and soothing on my own skin, preserving me forever, making me eternally beautiful.

"I thought of that. But I didn't care about too much anymore after he was taken away. And besides, I didn't want to have to stay Under when I got older. I can't live here again. This keeps me safe from that."

"You could have gone away. To the Desert. You can come with me now."

"I'm afraid. There weren't any heroes to take me away. Until you came."

"We'll go now."

"But why haven't we talked about it before? We both want Elysia. We can't help it. I couldn't even leave it to find him."

She pours more oil onto her palm. Liquid opal. Creamed pearl.

"Didn't she say not to use too much?"

"It feel so good. Like being kissed. Try some."

"What did she say about getting sleepy?"

"It makes you sleep. It's all right. We just have to get home before we fall asleep. We have time. We'll leave right now. I'm only using a little now anyway. When I get home, I'll put on more."

She begins to close the bottle. Then she looks at me. "Do you want some?"

The music is so loud and the smoke is getting inside of me. I feel old and withered from being down here, my face dry and hard enough to shatter. I want to forget the man in the boat with the hacked-up face, the tortured bodies outside this door. I could just try a little.

Like being kissed. By Paul. Like being kissed by Paul. The cells healing, my face a surface of pearl silk milk petals. I close my eyes and see the slanted eyes of the goddess of love and beauty, eyelashes hung with tiny crystals, irises like oasis pools full of water lilies.

A sweet peace comes over me. Perhaps it is like this after someone has made love to you and, skin still slick with him, you fall asleep in the warm of his body.

We hear a pounding on the door of the tiny room.

"Let's leave now," I say.

"Don't fall asleep." I speak to Arcadie as if she were a child. "Stay with me now."

She nods, digging her nails into her palm, blinking her eyes.

We have collapsed onto the shore of the river. She has taken more of the beauty oil and is rubbing in into her face, her throat, with ecstasy. Her breath comes heavy.

"Stop. Don't use any more." It is hard for me to speak. My eyelids ache. As if lashes hung with jewels. Drowning in sleep.

Drowning. Drowning. Drowning.

The river that steals your voice.

On the shore of the river I lay my body down. On the shore of the river of the river underground. I lay my body I lay my body down. On the shore of the river of the river underground.

Is this the last song ever I shall sing?

When I awake the first thing I am aware of is the bitter taste. My head is pressed to the damp and oozing dirt that lies along the river. My mouth beside a puddle. I wipe my hand across my lips. They are wct. A dark, greasy, reddish liquid streaks my skin. I spit the cold, congealed, tainted saliva from the depths of my throat.

No! I shout. But nothing comes out.

Arcadie. I reach for her hand. So cold. And I can hear the river whispering, singing a song.

all of the water fountains
shook and the water

128

poured down
you can hear a white sugar moth
its strange curiosity
fills your mind while
birds fly about
butter scotches
and grass that hummers back

My song. The song of my childhood. The river
has it.

I open my mouth. There is nothing. Raw gasps
only.

In the distance I see the light of the boat ap-
proaching the shore and hear the boat man's
whistle. We must get back. I try to make Arcadie
sit up. The glass jar, empty of oil now, falls from
her hand and shatters on a rock.

The river sings, "What matters except that we
shine like taffeta in the strange river light of
drugged houses candles in pink smoked glass?"

I remember the dead mermaid like an omen.
Arcadie is that pale—pale as the underbelly of a
dying fish. She glistens with the opalescent oil.
She will have no lines of age. She will have no
moles or scars. She will be sealed up white and
perfect like the machine of my mother.

night night come through the mirror
with your drugs that paint red lace on the
white walls

with your bundle of nasturtiums and violets
cut out the pain that lodges like a gnarled
  white root
in my rib cage

"Let go of her," voices are saying.
No. No.
But they can't hear me.
"She is dead. Let us take her."
A group of old people have gathered around. I cannot see their faces—only their sorrowful eyes, their twisted hands with the knob knuckles.

One of them is kneeling beside Arcadie, holding her wrist. The others shake their heads. The boat man spits into the river.

"You must get back. We'll take care of her," a man says.

I lunge forward, pressing my head to Arcadie's chest. It seems hollow. Her heartbeat and my voice both silenced.

"She used too much of Aphrodite's Oil."

"Go back." One of the old people presses a cold coin into my hand. Someone helps me to stand up. I look at the girl lying on the shore.

Lily daughter. Horse-man's lover. Beauty. Broken beauty smeared with a goddess' tears. I have nothing to give to you now. In the exile of my silence in this underground world I am more self-

ish than I have ever been. I do not even have a
song left to give.

I want to find River and go home. I want my
mother. I want the flowers. I want to bleed and
sing. There is only the river:

> *I dance papa*
> *I'm dancing*
> *I'm dancing up hills evermore*
> *I love my heart I can dance*
> *la la la la la la*
> *I have to dance*
> *I have a flute evermore*
> *I love to sing and dance*

CALLIOPE

I have wandered rough the sand dunes where
there are no people, no tents, not even the skele-
tons of trees. Will our home become a wasteland
like this one without her?

Where is my child? Where has she gone?

The lands are dying.

Rafe tries to work the hard ground, tries to
plant new seeds there. But the ground cracks
into lines like the ones on my face and nothing
rises up.

Paul makes poultices and teas from the herbs
we dried at harvest, but even as the sick drink

they shiver, not only from fever but in fear, for are these the last medicines they will ever have?

Dionisio mourns; he feels that if he had been stronger for Primavera none of this would have happened.

We all weep, but our tears are not strong enough charms to bring the clear rain. Our sweat is not a sorcerer's spell to fill the riverbeds. All our incense fires do not bring back the sun. We could roll a burning wheel down a hill and the sky would still be gray. Dionisio, Paul, and Rafe try to make music but no flowers grow. I cannot play any music at all.

So I left in the night. I took the old car and went out where the angry rocks scowl and grimace. I still remember the way to Elysia. There are no visions to guide me, but I feel she must have gone there.

It frightens me to go back to this place. After we left to find Rafe, I told myself I would never go back.

Now I have to cover my face with my cloak. I avoid the mirrors that are everywhere, reminding me that I no longer belong in this land of unlined youth. As I pass an entrance to Under I feel its pull—down.

"This is where you belong," sing the underworld voices. "Old One. Old One."

I belonged in Elysia once. It is hard to believe that now. I remember walking proudly down these streets, my hair woven through with amethyst grapes and green velvet leaves. I felt trembling, expectant. I knew something was going to happen that night. And it did; I met Dionisio. I remember dancing with him on the turning carousel. He was all curls and grinning mouth, his shirt open, his bare, sculptured chest. We drank so much wine that night. Love's blood, he said. My heart contracted and released in spasms the way my body would, later, in my bed.

So young then.

Now my beloved and I are too weary with grief to touch, even to make our music.

I remember the first time we all played together in Elysia as Ecstasia. Paul was more stern than usual that evening. He had on a white-gold damask shirt, the same color as his hair. He wouldn't sit still, sucking cigarette after cigarette, dashing them out when they burned down to his fingers. I wasn't so afraid, though. I knew that with a man like that in front of me on stage hardly anyone would notice what I was doing. I think Dionisio felt the same way. He was grinning like a little boy, but he did swallow a lot of wine right before we went on. Rafe was nervous. He said he thought Paul would dismember him if he missed a beat. There was so much tension between them then. And then all those years of love. Before I left the Desert, I heard the old harshness in their voices again.

Dionisio and I haven't made love since she left, either. We've all changed. I remember when we were so wild, after a show usually, that I thought we would all end up in the same bed. When we played music together it was almost like that anyway. We all desired each other with a kind of frenzy that we expressed through our instruments. And weren't our instruments our bodies at those times? Sometimes I think that in a way Primavera is the child of all of us, born as much from that intercourse of music as from my body and Dionisio's meeting in the purple darkness.

This is one of the nightclubs where we used to play. The thick glass of the windows distorts the shapes behind, making the people into ghosts.

It is so bright inside that I can hardly see. Hopefully it is too bright for the costumed dancers to see the old woman who has entered. The music is as harsh as the light. It is nothing like we used to play.

I look around, trying to find someone who I can ask about my daughter, someone who would not shun me. Oh, where are my visions now? I feel like a person who has slowly grown blind, so slowly that sometimes she forgets she ever saw at all, but then—suddenly—reminded of the aching absence of her sight. The absence of my bond to Primavera's mind.

"Excuse me," I say to a tall woman in red, "have

you seen a young woman who can sing . . . she can make flowers grow . . . when she sings there are flowers?" I take out the tiny painting, the portrait of a beautiful face peering from a torrent of dark hair.

The woman blinks her eyes at me. Her eyelashes look sharp enough to cut glass. So do her teeth. I can see blue veins under the thin white sheath of her skin that may rip at any moment from a stroke of eyelash.

"Gone," the woman says, brushing the air with her hand. A look of great distaste. "Under, I heard. You should be there too by now, don't you think?"

I draw my hood closer over my head and run out into the street.

Under.

If there is anywhere I dread more than the barren wastelands, more than Elysia, it is Under. I saw my own mother perish there in a room of dying Old Ones; I confronted the horror of my father there and almost died imprisoned by the demon he had become beneath the earth. When Rafe and Paul and Dionisio came back to free the Old Ones I did not join them. We all decided I should stay with Primavera in case anything happened to them. Though I was afraid to let them go without me, I was also relieved. That place is every nightmare I have ever known.

* * *

But now I am back again.

Just as this world is the opposite of what sings and shines in paradise, here I am the opposite of the Calliope who could once fill the world with song and sustenance.

Now I see that self walking toward me from the boat that has arrived at the shore. My own face young, my own eyes empty. She is singing to herself in a dead monotone.

"Have I forgotten no I remember though I have tried to burn it to embers the night when the one in the skeleton mask ripped at my heart while he kissed my mouth the night when the one with the fingers that pry opened my rib cage and buried inside."

Ecstasia's old song. She stops and stares at me with glassy eyes in a replica of my own youthful head.

"You've come back," she says. "You are older now."

"I am looking for my daughter."

"I didn't think you'd ever come back."

"Neither did I. I thought I passed the test. I thought I had made enough descents."

"Then there will be one more," she says. "Always another one. Unless you are already dead like I am."

"But you didn't want to stay up there when you had the chance."

"No. This is where I live."

"What do you do here?" I think of being underground forever. This could have been me if she hadn't come down to switch places and let me back up.

"I make Aphrodite Oil. Doctor's recipe. Beauty from the hungry plants and the fat old ugly roots. I make Aphrodite Oil. Is that why you came? Want some?"

"No. I am looking for my daughter."

"Come with me."

I feel like a machine myself. Instead of getting onto the waiting boat, I follow her along the near shore but away from the tunnel that leads back up.

We are going into a kind of forest. It is all a tangle of roots that snake down, grasping for sustenance and, finding nothing but poison, grow bloated and then rot.

Once I dreamed of forests full of gentle spirits and healing plants. The spirits were clothed in moss and star flowers; they flew like sunbeams, shook like laughter through the branches, or emerged as glistening crystal tears from secret pools. The plants could ease burns, cleanse, even make the old young again and revive the dead; they grew in the shapes of temples and glowed with light and warmth when night came cool, swayed their leaves like fans in the heat of day. This was the place in my mind where visions were born. Now the forest is a nightmare, the antithesis of the magic one, the way I have become the antithesis of my lost self. These roots would blister, infect, corrupt; they would wither young flesh early and destroy all life.

The threadlike tips of the roots that dangle down from above graze my cheek. The creature reaches up and plucks them, dropping them into her basket.

"Your daughter came wanting some Aphrodite Oil."

I hide my shaking hands against my cloak. "What? You saw her?"

"I could never have a daughter. You have a beautiful daughter. She was little and now she is big. I stay always the same."

"Where is she?"

"She came looking for Aphrodite Oil. I gave it to her and she promised to come back and visit me. Did she promise? I hope she comes back. But you're here now. Come walk with me. I'm gathering. I will give you something to make you look like me again."

"No. Tell me about Primavera."

There is the sudden sound of footsteps; the creature vanishes behind a cascade of roots.

"Get away from the path. They're coming."

I follow her into a dank darkness. I can feel roots trying to twist themselves around my arms. All I can think of is that she, the image of my young self, has seen Primavera.

"Tell me!"

"Must be silent now. Homunculi."

Through the tangle I see a parade of small men coming down the path carrying metal tools as big as they are. None of them stand taller than my knee and their faces are black with soot. Some have long snouts or huge pointed ears, protruding teeth, missing eyes.

"Homunculi," she whispers. "They're going mining in the Rock. The man came from above and bought a metal collar from them. He awaits his new bride."

The little men seem to be marching through my gut and I feel that I will vomit up whatever remains in my stomach. I want to silence the creature who stands beside me chattering softly. I hate her for possessing my youth and for not understanding. But I must remember that once this creature saved my life and the life of my daughter when we were imprisoned underground. Now, perhaps, her clues will lead me to Primavera.

"Where is she?" The small men have passed by.

"In Under."

"We are Under. Where?"

"Somewhere across the river. Maybe the boat man knows."

I lunge out of our hiding place and reel down the path, back the way we came. The roots try to clasp my arms, the fibrous tips lash and scratch my eyes, and I flail against them. My feet are treading backwards in mud like I am on a nightmare hike.

"Come back and stay with me." I hear my own voice wail, but distorted as if through metal tubes.

Finally I stumble out of the forest, but the oppressive Under world is no relief, for here the forest is not of roots but palpitating darkness and a low dirt roof caving in from above.

I stand at the riverbank.

> *finding all the bunnerbuds*
> *fossils and the procadillys*
> *shine and glitter while we dance*
> *spangles of the sea stars*
> *the ocean fligs and flatters*
> *but by any chance the mushroom grows*
> *there is green moss under the heather*
> *once again when biddle webs sleep*
> *between the flowers*
> *the green moss has grown*
> *to be yellow and now all*
> *the plants have grown*
> *to be crystal*
> *the trees glitter . . . green . . .*
>
> *it is good for me and him*
> *always to be in the grass lying down*

> *feeling each other's warm*
> *if you are a grownup*
> *you can still*
> *do anything*
> *you can smell things*
> *and look at things and*
> *hear things upon your ears*

"Primavera!" I cry. I have found you! Primavera.

But the voice is strange, muffled, dim, watery as if drowning. I stare into the foul red river. It is the river, not my child, that sings.

I fall to my knees in the mud. I want to plunge into those waters to find the imposter, to wring the throat that tries to imitate my daughter.

"What have you done with her?"

The boat man is standing in the prow of his boat staring down at me. He spits into the river.

"Who you looking for? Everyone's always looking for someone down here." He laughs and I see the rot of his teeth.

His mouth. I see a flash of tunnel. My first memory of the tunnel that brought me down here. Decay. Then the image is gone.

I show him the portrait. He spits again.

"Far as I know that one's dead. Another Addict, though. Not much of a loss."

"No!" I scream.

But the river is still singing Primavera's song, taunting me.

Yes. Yes.

PAUL

I remember how my skin first broke out in those hot red welts. I tried to walk with my head up but I felt all the eyes on me, on my face. Once I had been stared at for other reasons.

I had been a really beautiful child. Grown women fell in love with me. When I first left the outpost where I had been raised and came to Elysia I had skin like a flower's white petals. With my perfect skin and my songs I left the house full of suffocating women. I left my mother. They called her Pearl because all the women in the house used the names of jewels, but her real name was Paradisia so in a way I left paradise too, just like Primavera, to find the clear hard brilliance of the city. I knew I wanted to start a band.

But I became monstrous. I wonder now, was it that I felt I *was* a monster because I loved men—I loved men and I wasn't a woman. And so my beauty was not what I deserved. I should look like who I was—deformed. My face swelled up. If I bent down it hurt like there were pebbles in my flesh. I couldn't sleep with my cheeks against the pillows; I had to lie on my back. I'd go to the mirror and see the feverish boils ready to burst, gauging out their deep pockets so that even when I healed there would be these scars.

People say I'm a handsome man now. Good bones. Eyes so bright they hiss, Rafe says. I don't know. I still feel like that blistering boy sometimes. I can't forget him.

I'm surprised they didn't force me Under with that skin. If you could call it skin. It was some kind of a battleground. But I didn't go Under. I wore a hood, I moved quietly. My eyes were full of violence. I kept singing. I learned to play guitar.

Have you heard Paul? they asked each other. The shame began to dissolve. The music began to change everything. I sang the demons out of my body into Elysia. My face cooled.

This city reminds me of that time.

On these streets I am again the boy who pretended to wear his scars like a shield although they were just as much the bleeding wound. I am the boy—although then I didn't think of myself as a boy; by Elysia's standards I was getting older—who wanted to start a band that would make everyone love me. And I wanted Rafe.

I had seen him in front of the stage watching me sing. There were so many gorgeous boys around Elysia, all dressed up in their bright costumes, but this one was different. He looked like he was about to cry. His jaw was set, very hard, as if he were trying not to let it show, but his eyes were melting. I howled and whispered the song as if I were coming, my mouth against a lover's ear. I remember the stage seemed to sway like a wave—I was surfing my desire.

Rafe. I never thought I'd touch him. I wanted to cut the wanting out of myself. It was like when my skin first erupted, that sense of torturing my body from the inside out.

Primavera on the rock that night of the moon festival. She reminded me of me—wanting someone you can't have, hating yourself for it. But she is stronger than I ever was. She'll be all right. Many men will love her.

I wonder if anyone ever looked at me at that time in this city and thought, Paul will be all right, many men will love him, he will recognize his beauty and stop hating himself.

If they said that to me I would have hated them, not believed them, and besides I didn't want many men, only Rafe.

So now Rafe is my lover. But when I left the Desert we did not even embrace.

"I am going to find Calliope," I told him.

"I'm going with you."

"No," I said, "it's better you wait here. The people need you."

"Dionisio will stay."

144

"They need you, too, Rafe. I have to go find her."

He looked angry, his eyes hooded and his lips pressed together until all their softness and color were gone.

"What?" I demanded.

"Are you going to find Calliope or Primavera?"

"What do you mean?"

"You want Primavera back."

"Yes, of course. Don't you?"

"Paul!" he shouted. "What has happened to us?"

At any other time I would have thrown my arms around him until our backs ached with it and our blood lunged through our veins so we could not distinguish our pulse from each other's. But I didn't want to touch him—the man I would have died for at any moment all these years. I felt like the dying lands around me and all I wanted to do was leave. Yes, I wanted Primavera back, but what was he saying to me?

"You love her," he said. "You desire her. I thought I could take it. But I sit here every day pounding at the earth, pounding at my drum skins, and it's all hollow. I can't take it. She is gone and we don't touch anymore. I want her back, too, but it terrifies me. Is she all the power there is?"

I love you, Rafe, and I want us all to be together. I could have said it. She is not going to be my lover when she comes back.

But my words had dried up and I just stared at him.

"I am going because Calliope might be in danger. And I will try to find Primavera, too."

I feel our barrenness. What are we doing—two men—we think we can create some fertile world? We can't even create life. What will happen to us as we get older and there are no children? Our bodies will deteriorate. We pretend we don't care, we're above that, out in our paradise where the old are still respected. But we are Elysia's children! Beauty is what we worship. Even Rafe looks less beautiful to me now. And how do I look to him?

On these cold streets, where the china dolls serve cocktails behind the flickering glass, all the children are possessed by beauty. It haunts their bodies like a spirit that will not stay forever though they think that now. Like a spirit it draws others to it and like a spirit it cannot be willfully, eternally possessed. The haunting perfume and whispering song of beauty. I am some old ghost hunter who thinks that I am here to rescue Primavera. Am I really looking for something else—some image of the young boy-Paul whose songs palpitated with life, who could rescue souls with music and, though he couldn't give birth to a child, carried life in his music? Perhaps on these streets I am looking for an unscarred Paul.

I will go to the circus.

The circus is where Rafe met Lily. I hated Lily. She was everything I wanted to be and wasn't and would never be. So how could Rafe love her? How could I bear Rafe loving her? Then Lily died from that Orpheus drug and it felt like my lover had died. It wasn't just that I was feeling Rafe's pain because I loved Rafe. I really felt the loss of the girl who could walk on air. I remembered her watching Rafe play, looking at him over a bouquet of flowers as pink and white and fragrant as she was. I was surprised because I had thought I never really felt for Lily, but she was in me, too.

Now I'm at the circus where Lily used to walk the tightrope. It seems almost deserted now. The centaurs are gone and the bird-women. I have often wondered about those creatures—what it must have been like for them entertaining the crowds of all-human beauties in a city where anything imperfect was so despised. I wondered how long they would last.

Today three boys in white are practicing an acrobatic routine. They each have two arms, two legs, delicate little bodies, doll-like faces. They can bend and twist themselves into impossible inhuman contortions and then come out of these smiling and perfect again. Elysia must love them.

Just a brief reminder of what *can* go wrong with the body and then—don't panic—everything is fine again.

For some reason seeing the beautiful boys gives me a chill and I walk outside the tent and stand surveying the landscape of gray sky and cobblestone streets.

A light drizzle has begun to fall but my hood is already up—no reason these pretty children should see an old man's face. I guess that's what I have.

Suddenly I have also this great desire to see the place where Rafe, Callie, Dionisio, and I lived.

My legs move me through the spiraling streets, twisting alleys. Remember wandering here alone, dreaming up songs. *There in the city that denies destruction all of them waiting for love's . . .* What was the word? Is my mind going?

I'd walk here dreaming of Rafe. He used to run these streets—never still, he was always racing away from something. Speed-child he called himself. But since Primavera left, I find him sitting for hours at a time gazing out across the diminishing gardens. Strange, though, I can't see his face now. It used to fill up my head as if it were imprinted on my skull beneath my own cartilage and flesh.

The songs and the dreams of my lover are gone.

As the band Ecstasia we'd drive these streets to our shows with all our instruments. Those where high times. High—I haven't used that word in ages. We felt flushed and quickened knowing we'd be on the stage soon with those young and dazzled faces reflecting back our light. We loved to perform, but then we didn't know the power of music, the ancient miracles of singing the name and calling forth gardens with the pounding pulse of drum, the healing fingers of keys, the rib cages of guitar full of heart, the dreams made manifest in the voice. Did we do all this? We are all silent now in paradise without Miss Spring, and is she silent, too?

On this journey I have seen no sign of her flowers. Unlike us—her family—who strained to learn how to make magic and could only make it together and only where the danger or the love was vast enough, Primavera was practically born singing flowers all by herself. She doesn't need me or any of us. Why am I following her? No—it's Calliope I'm following. She may need me. But I also hope to find her daughter and bring her back with us to the gardens corroding to desert again and the hearts that are doing the same.

I catch sight of my reflection in the glass walls of a bar. Fiery lights inside the place cast an orange glow on my skin, but this doesn't hide that my face is not a boy's anymore. It somehow shocks me now—is this me? I don't feel like this and you can begin to see the perpetual grin of skull. I need to get out of Elysia. Here I was in torment as a youth with that erupting skin and now as an old man with this skin wrinkling. In the Desert we love our bodies and our faces—all kinds. The clear water soothes the lines and scars; the fresh air, the moist soil, the petals drifting, the bird songs—all this heals and reminds us that we have bodies only to love and live and then to be drawn back into the earth and reborn to nature. At least that's how it was while Primavera was still with us.

Here in Elysia there is no cycle. You are born and you eat sweets, wear pretty clothes; you get older, you go Under, and you die.

Our loft. When we left, we left everything and we didn't lock the doors. We didn't plan on coming back.

I go upstairs and look through the windows. It seems empty. I try the door. It's open. I walk softly inside. No one around.

This place has changed. I remember our lush velvets and our urns of incense, silk flowers. On the wall I can still make out the faded silver garden. We always knew we wanted gardens.

We moved in here when the band had started

to be a success. We were so proud of our loft. I had been in a tiny one-room place across town with just a mat on the floor and a hot plate. I hid there. It was dark, no windows. When my face healed I wanted to get away from there. It was haunted by gargoyles with boils on their cheeks.

Callie and Rafe had their parents' place, but they were almost never at home—too many memories. Dionisio, who had come from the outpost with me, was wandering around, staying with whomever would let him sleep on their floor until he met Callie and moved in with her. But we all needed to be together. We needed space and warmth and a place without memories. I suppose you always have to keep moving to avoid that.

When we moved into the loft I thought, Rafe will be sleeping in the room next to me—how will I sleep? But how could I turn down such a thing, to have him so near? And besides it would bring us all together as Ecstasia. We could practice all the time in our small paradise where nothing grew but silk flowers, painted flowers and our music, which would someday—we didn't know then—become a beautiful girl-child who could sing real flowers.

Now it looks like some children have taken over this place. Dirty mats and torn blankets everywhere. Cigarette packs, empty bottles, cans, newspaper wads. When we were in Elysia no one lived like this. It looks like these children really needed a roof over their heads.

I listen at the door of my room—silence—and I enter. The gold sun clock is gone. Of course. That was the one thing I had really wanted to take, but time is different in the Desert. We don't need time. In Elysia you have to count off every moment knowing you'll be going Under soon. But the children who live here now might not have wanted to think about Under and they probably needed whatever food the clock could buy.

Heaps of trash in this room now. Here is where, wanting Rafe, I thrashed against the mattress, masturbating myself to limp despair. I shudder at the memory. How weak. And here I wept when Rafe almost died from the drug Orpheus which brought Lily back. I thought, if he dies I'll go down and get some Orpheus too, just to see him again, maybe touch him in death. I wondered—wonder still—does the Orpheus vision stay true to the dead one's soul or fulfill the fantasy of the person who takes it? Because possibly Rafe won't want me even then but at least I will have seen him again, I thought.

He didn't die. He healed. He made love with me. He went off to the Desert. We found him. He is my lover now. I must remember who I am, but being back here I become the frightened, angry Paul gripping himself in the night until his semen came like blood.

I shouldn't be here anymore. No beautiful music remains in these rooms. No Ecstasia ghost. Just silence. Just as well. But we're not singing in the Desert, either.

Deep down I'm afraid that maybe we'll never play again. I have no songs in me now anyway. Primavera. Why this silence? Separated from my loved ones and my love for music. Freezing in Elysia. That could have been a song, but I wouldn't know how to begin.

My throat is so dry but I don't want the water in my flask. I should save it, right? Yes, save it. And a little Elysia champagne might help me do what I have to do. Because if Calliope and Primavera aren't here they might be underground. Maybe I'll try a bar, but I'm not sure I'm brave enough to go inside.

"Hey! Old One! What are you doing here?"

The children are standing in the doorway. Why didn't I even think about this happening? It was as if this place was still mine. And I'm usually so wary. That's what comes from living in shame for so long, but I stumbled right into this one.

I try to put up my hood, mumbling something about sorry to disturb you lost my way on the way out of town sorry sorry.

They are moving closer toward me, here in my

own room. Once of them is a very handsome boy with dark slick hair and bare, lean, muscular arms. He's just the type I would have lusted for when I lived here. Maybe he would have met me in a bath or an alley or even taken me to his bed when I was young. Now I disgust him. But he smiles a sex-grin anyway.

"Ooh maybe the Old One came looking for some fresh-flesh to suck on."

He starts toward me. I feel the rise of fear. The others are close behind.

"What are you doing in Elysia?" the boy whispers. "Don't you know better?" He puts out his hand as if to caress my neck and I pull away, fumbling for my knife.

A smaller boy comes forward, staring at me from under shaggy hair. "Why are you in our house?" he says.

The dark boy pushes him back without turning away from me. "Shut up, Simon. Go call Cam."

The small boy won't move. He keeps staring.

A bigger boy comes into the room. He has a thick face like his fists. "What's happening?"

The handsome dark boy says, "Cam, want to help me do this Old One? He wandered right in here on a flesh hunt."

"Wrong place," the one called Cam says. "We'll hunt his flesh but not like he likes it."

"He's a Same-Sexer," someone else says. "And Old!"

They all start making coughing, sputtering, gagging sounds.

I look around frantically. I pull out my knife, but I don't know how it will help me now.

Cam and the dark boy grab my arms and Cam uses his free hand to press my throat closed. I feel the insides of my neck like pulp. I drop the knife.

They push me against the wall. The wall where my gold sun clock once hung.

I close my eyes. Maybe it is right that I die now. The things I love are so far away and fading. At least I lived in paradise. I didn't die Under. I saw Primavera grow up. I had Rafe my beloved my Rafe. Forgive me my beloved for not holding you before I left. For not being able to see your face.

I try to see Rafe's face, remembering the way his cheekbones felt.

I can feel my own knife blade, a slice of cold at my throat.

This is the throat that once sang.

If I could even sing for them would they recognize Paul's voice, the voice of Ecstasia? Once it was the voice of enchantment.

"Paul."

My name. I am waking from this dream?

The small boy, Simon, has pushed forward again.

"It's Paul," he says. "Ecstasia! It's Paul."

"Paul?" The two bigger boys hesitate, glaring at my face. "Shut up, Simon."

"No. It is. It's him. I have his picture."

Everything is a blur but I can hear rustling and sense the child scrambling through piles of papers searching for something.

"Come on, Starl," Cam snaps at the dark-haired boy. But there is a difference in both of their eyes now. As if they are looking, waiting to make sure.

"If you are Paul Ecstasia, then you'd better sing for us. Fast!" shouts Starl.

I imagine how it would have been years before, him in the audience watching me with wet lips, hot for something different than what drives him now. But my throat is parched. Old like my face.

"Sing 'Underground.' That's where you belong. 'Once I had a dream woke me from my sleep now I've lost her in a nightmare but I'm going to find her somewhere even if it takes me down under underground.' That's where you belong Old One."

"Don't give him the words. He'll try to pretend he's Paul."

"Everyone in Elysia knows those words, boy. But no one can sing like Paul did."

Simon squeezes in between the two bigger

boys. He is holding something in his hand. He gives it to Cam.

"Paul is young, you ash-brain," Cam says.

"He wouldn't be anymore. Right, Starl? Look."

Starl lowers his eyes. He has long lashes. He looks so different with the lids soft over the hate in his pupils. I feel the sweat drip down the sides of my body like someone's saliva.

"It does look like him," Starl says.

I glimpse the photograph as Starl hands it to Cam. It's of me with my guitar between my legs. My erection. I remember Rafe taking the picture. I didn't think I was beautiful then but now I see.

"It's Paul," Simon breathes again. "*The* Paul."

"Sing then, Paul." Cam palms his fist. He can already hear my screams and feel the sudden split and sink of knife into my flesh. I can see it in his eyes.

My voice is cracked. My heart is cracked. I've forgotten everything.

"Sing 'Ecstasia.' " Simon's voice.

> *together we can sow and breed*
> *from the tiny husk of seed*
> *our own flower in the weeds*
> *it tears the sky until it bleeds*
> *clouds melt to rain, milk, semen, sea*
> *ecstasia the ecstasy*

> *dreaming eyelids trembling*
> *in our garden of delirium*
> *music still our bodies binding*
> *to the whirling willow wind*
> *amethyst stained mist of sea*
> *ecstasia the ecstasy*

So the song "Ecstasia" sings itself. Or close to what it used to be. Maybe the words get tangled and I miss some notes. But I become Paul for them and for myself for a moment. I am an Old One but Paul.

They back away. They stand dazed.

"Paul, why did you come back?" Simon has pressed in close to me now as Starl and Cam move away. "Where's Ecstasia?"

"I have to get back to them," I mumble, seeing my chance. I start to push toward the door before the sight of my aged face makes them forget the song.

"Wait, Paul. Sing some more."

"No. I'm leaving. I don't belong here anymore."

"You sure don't, Old One!" someone calls. I don't turn to see who.

"Get out of here. Run, Old One."

They laugh but they sound weary now. I quicken my pace as I push out the front door of what was once our loft. I run down the steps into the street, my legs ready to collapse with trembling.

There are footsteps behind me.

"Paul. Paul. Wait."

"Simon, thank you. Leave me now."

"Paul, I've always loved Ecstasia. I want to be just like you."

"Leave me, Simon. They don't want you to talk to me."

"Can I help you? Why are you here?"

I pause for a moment and turn to him. He keeps pushing the hair out of his eyes. The skin on his cheeks is a little broken out. He is barefoot.

"Have you seen any other Old Ones around here lately?" I ask.

"I don't think people should treat them so bad just cause they're Old Ones. Or Same-Sexers. Why are people so mean about that stuff?"

"They're afraid, Simon. Just tell me if you saw anyone who was older in the last few days."

"Yes. There was a woman in the streets yesterday. She was asking about the girl who sings flowers."

"Tell me about them both."

"The girl who sings flowers came here and started singing and there were jewels and stuff. Then the old woman came looking for her. I heard they both went Under. Do you know them, Paul?"

159

"I can't talk to you anymore. Thank you for saving me, Simon. Go on."

I hurry into an alley. I will have to go Under. I don't have time to stop for a drink and I can't take the chance anyway. After what just happened maybe maybe Under won't seem so bad. Or maybe it will be worse.

I have reached the opening in the street. This is the way Under.

"Paul . . ."

The boy still. I sigh and turn to him. "If you wait for me here I can take you into the Desert with me when I go back. It's not paradise right now there, but no one treats you badly if you aren't just like them."

Simon pushes the hair out of his eyes again. "I'm too scared, Paul."

"All right. But you can think about it. If you ever want to you can come out there."

"Thank you, Paul Ecstasia."

I reach out and put my hand on his shoulder before I descend.

She is lying on the shore like a dead tree. I fall to my knees beside her and touch her cheek. I have faced the loss of our Spring; I have stopped touching my lover; I have almost died. I survived all those, but this I cannot bear. This would be too much. Not Calliope. She is the only one who can hold us all together. Hold what remains of our world together. My tears fall onto her, the first tears I remember setting free in years.

She opens her eyes, once so full with vision and tenderness; they are now almost empty.

"I can't live without her," she says.

"Calliope, come back. I will bring you back."

"My daughter."

I know I shouldn't ask yet, but she sees the question in my face.

"She is dead."

"How do you know? Did you see?" I feel a surge of fury. "Who told you that?"

"The boat man."

"He doesn't know. She made the choice to leave us. Come with me now. We'll go home. She'll find us."

Suddenly I hate Primavera for doing this to us—for leaving, for destroying her mother. Rafe and I may never be lovers again. I was almost killed. And what do we have to return to but a dying land? I just want to get away from here. I've been Under too many times for one man. Once to find the drug to make Rafe love me. Once to rescue Rafe. Once to bring the Old Ones up. This is too much. After awhile you never return. I feel the darkness collapsing in around me, stealing my senses.

I pull Calliope up from the mud and shake her. Her feet slip and slide as I hold her shoulders. Her hair and cloak are caked with mud.

"We are going now. She made her choice."

"There is nothing left," says Calliope.

CALLIOPE

I cannot see her anywhere in my mind. But I am crowded crowded crowded with other visions.

Paul is driving me through the desert as if everything is all right. Doesn't he see?

All around us the demons are dancing.

The demons of Hunger are dancing in the desert.

Once there was food for everyone. Now look what has happened. The babies are caving in on themselves, inside out, starving. Flies swarm to their eyes. Their bones will tear through their wrinkled skin.

The serpent is licking my ears, telling me these tales. The babies are dying slowly while the Hunger demons dance around them gnashing brass teeth.

The demons of Disease are running with skulls on sticks. Fire burns inside the skulls, flickering behind the cavernous eyes, nostrils, the gape-jaws. Men and women with purple landscapes on their flesh lie in the leering shadows cast by the skull torches. They will not touch each other. They will not make love. Blood and semen, once the potions of life, are poison now, poison as the smoky air, poison as the fluorescent burning rain.

The serpent is licking my ear. He will slip his long tongue deep into my ear, then his whole worm body. He will bury himself inside my skull to tell me these things.

The demons of War are ravaging the earth. They are slicing open her belly with their metal penises and aborting the life in her. They are burning off her hair. They are sucking the fluids from her veins. They are chopping off her breasts and her hands.

Am I seeing visions of our past? Of our future? Perhaps both.

When we lived in Elysia, we pretended these things were never real, would never be real. When we created our paradise, we remembered for a moment but we vowed, never again. Now I see clearly all the things I have run from all my life. My visions, which once helped me to find and save the ones I love, are now a bleeding scream of memory or prophecy I cannot heal.

4. GUNN

Primavera's only ornament is River's feather necklace that she has put on again. She leaves Elysia on her motorcycle. It is like dropping off the edge of the world into an abyss of sand and dark. Soon the tinkling carousel music is lost in the wind.

But as she ventures farther Primavera sees four glass towers splintering beams of light across the sand.

She remembers the stories Paul and Dionisio had told her about the outpost where they grew up. The house full of beautiful women and riches. This is that place, she is sure. It calls to her almost as if a voice wailed from the towers, "Come, come, Primavera. Find your flowers here." Paul's voice, perhaps. She knows she must see the place where Paul grew up, the courtyard where he played, the hallways he wandered, where he lay at night wrapped in the shame of his secret love for men—here in this house of women—the way she lay for years in the torment of her love for him. She will leave right after this, she tells herself. She will find the feathered boy and take him with her back to paradise. Maybe there her family will give her back her voice. Maybe the water of the Sound will hear her.

There is a vast jade wall around the house. She gets off her bike and walks through the gateway into the courtyard. It is full of trees and flowers that look like the ones she once sang, but these are hard and cold and will never die. The leaves and stems are green glass, the blossoms, pink and blue crystal. There is a soft tinkling sound like wind chimes, but it is the trees themselves. Some of the flowers flash on and off, lighting the garden.

She leaves her motorcycle and goes to the pink marble doorway. The door opens when she touches it, and she is in a corridor with a high ceiling. It is very quiet here. She thinks she should be able to hear the music and laughter of women filling this place. Even the echo of the phantom-Paul's voice is silent now. There is only the sound of her own feet in the metal and leather boots on the mosaic tiles.

How long does she wander? It feels like hours. The rooms are of different colored marble with

intricate mosaic floors. Round orbs give off a silvered light. Finally she comes to a central courtyard.

And here, among more glassy trees and flowers,
enclosed by a wall painted with fading images of
dancing women whose faces have peeled away,
here in the center of this strange place she finds
the cages.

And in the cages, the creatures.

Part of her feels horror.

Sometimes she has imagined what it would be
like to fly, to live in the river, to run like a horse.
She has dreamed of that freedom, that power,
and fears the wildness in herself that wants to
live as beasts live, moved purely by need and desire. She has felt torn between the heat of her
limbs and the thoughts in her mind telling her to
be careful and good and always calm.

Don't scream or cry, don't run to him and
throw yourself at his feet, pleading for him to
take you in his arms, don't strip off your clothes
and run naked to the water wild with wanting.

But what of these creatures who are half animal, half human? How do they feel the tearing?
she wonders. Is it a physical thing like a wound
where human torso meets that other part? How
does it cage their souls? And here they are caged
again in these large gold and silver domes. They
are unnaturally silent. She has known music and
laughter all through her life. Where she was born

the birds sang, every creature had a song. But this courtyard is so full of silence it is like a thing, another being, also caged. And the eyes watch, from behind the scrolls and bars, full of a pain that she has never seen or even imagined.

Bird-women. They have mournful faces and sharp-looking, narrow breasts; they have streaming wisps of hair. But their lower bodies are feathery swells that narrow into thin bird legs and clawed, hectic feet that scrape the cage floors. Some have pale plumage, others dark, but none of them look capable of any flight. There is something pinched and cluttered about their faces, almost as if they are hiding small beaks beneath their lips. One lifts a scaled leg to scratch herself, then bows her head with a kind of shame. Shame is what Primavera sees here more than anything else. They cannot imagine themselves as creatures of enchantment, only as monsters.

The faunesses are wilder. Their round, dark eyes roll in their heads and some stamp their hooves. They have flat noses and plush lips and round brown breasts that seem to float on their rib cages, nipples upturned. Their goat legs look powerful enough to help them to escape. Maybe it is their thin human flesh and bare chilled breasts and vulnerable throats that keep them from thrashing against the bars in rage and crying out.

Cry out, she wants to tell them. Why are you like this in silence? But she understands. She cannot cry out, either. She feels her femaleness suddenly as a kind of horror that someone— whoever did this—would want to punish, leer at, despise, imprison. She feels swollen, bloated, hideous. She wants to hide.

In a glass tank in the center of the courtyard are the mermaids. They do not need bars. For how would they escape? And even if they could thrust themselves over the high, sleek wall of glass and flop onto the icy stone and pull themselves along with their human arms, drag their fleshy fishtails and scrape their bellies until they were out of this courtyard, then, what? If the front doors were not locked, even then, what would they find in the desert? Or even in the poison sea?

They stare at her through the glass, their eyes bulging slightly, greenish-blue as water. Their hair is that same color, making wreaths like the weeds that grow in the ponds where she is from. They look so thin; she can see every fine bone, between their small breasts, and of their ribs; they are crammed together in their tank, swished back and forth by the water, pressing their hands against the glass so the lineless palms look bleached white. The fish tails wave behind them, a myriad of rainbow scales that, even with such shimmering jewel-like beauty, cannot save them. Are, perhaps, the reason for this imprisonment.

She will be sick. She must leave.

She cannot leave. She must try to save them.

She cannot save them. She thinks, I am only a stupid girl who left paradise seeking what—adventure, adoration?

Then she hears her boots. For a moment she thinks she is walking but she isn't moving at all—she can't and besides these boots are heavier; and she knows the man when she sees his face.

The creatures cower in their cages.

"You've found me," he says. "The motorcycle always comes back here eventually."

It is Gunn. He is wearing the mirrored glass over his eyes.

Her throat hurts. If it hurt before because she was too full of life, now it is raw, racked, empty.

"Have you come to give us a little song?"

She turns to leave but he grabs her arm. His steel grip.

"Primavera. These are my Mutants. Aren't they fascinating? Everyone has a different preference, of course. I myself, though, won't sleep with any of them. I only like women. Beauties."

She remembers the words from the diary Arcadie showed her: "He pulled up my dress and stuck his body into me. I want to scrape my insides clean."

Gunn touches her shorn head. She pulls away. He grabs her other wrist. The only sound is glass leaves.

"I've been waiting for you. I knew you'd come eventually. I get sick of just these ugly beasts all day and night."

She opens her mouth, gasping like a fish without water.

"Trying to sing? That's all right. You're better silent. I like it quiet." He addresses the figures in the cages. "Right?"

He laughs, the lips so thin that the skin seems flayed.

Her body feels as if it is turning inside out. She tries to wrench away, but before she can move he has fastened a high collar around her neck.

"From the little men under the ground."

The cold metal almost strangles her. And as soon as this happens, she known that he does not need a cage to keep her. The collar at her throat is like shackles on all her limbs. Her head drops, the metal edge cutting against the flesh. He takes hold of a ring on the collar and drags her body behind him to his chambers. If she had even the memory of song in her, it is all gone now.

The room is a deep red. This is all she is really aware of—the pulsing red and the bed that could be upholstered in nails.

Her throat is constricted as if huge tumors grow there. She would cut them out if she could, but still she could not sing. She is a parched desert the way paradise was desert before her family came and played their music. But there is no music.

Later, when she thinks Gunn is asleep, she tries to get up. She hears his voice.

"You can run around the house all night, but you'll never get out. Others tried before."

The pain in her body writhes. She falls back down.

She stumbles through the house wearing the white gown with the metal band at the waist that squeezes her to a third of her size and makes her breasts and hips bulge out. The metal collar is still on her throat. She cannot breathe.

She never sees Gunn's body. Only the naked white hand. In the day she watches it as he gnaws on his fingers, goes from cage to cage checking on his creatures, eats his rare meat, fiddles with his many keys. The hand seems to have its own life. In her delirium she half expects it to speak. It would laugh, telling the inner darkness of her body to the day, telling of the vivid split of pain in her body. She almost wishes it would, so that someone would hear. But who? The tortured creatures in the cages? Their own pain makes them deaf to all else, as mute as she is.

He lets her wander like this, through the house. He knows she cannot escape through the locked doors, the stone walls, the gate. She is weak from not eating and from the bands on her body and from the pain.

She has come here before, to the courtyard. The creatures stare at her. She wonders if any of them can speak, but they are always silent.

Today, though, she hears soft moans drifting from one of the bird-women like molting feathers.

Primavera stands outside the cage. The bird-woman looks up—bright azure eyes with rounded lids half covering them. The eyes remind Primavera of something—someone—and she does not feel the revulsion in her stomach that she felt before. The creature stops crying and staggers to her feet, the thin legs unfolding from beneath the bird body.

"You must get away from here," the woman whispers. Her voice is rough with tears as it comes from her narrow throat.

Primavera sees a vision of a white horse in a field. Where did she see him first so long ago? she wonders. Then she sees a white horse's head nailed to a wall. Blood drips down like veins of marble.

Have you seen the loneliness of bird-women in cages, Paul? she thinks. Have you heard them silent? Have you heard them cry?

The bird-woman is still speaking. "I am Zephyra. Come to me if you need to talk. It is all we have."

If that is true, then she has nothing. She shakes her head wildly, gesturing to her throat.

"You cannot speak?"

Suddenly there is a sound of heaviness coming from the front of the house. The creatures flatten themselves against the far sides of their cages. Some whimper as if they have been struck.

"The giants," Zephyra says. "Go away. Hide."

Before she can, Gunn enters. With him are three huge men. They have to stoop to get through the archway into the courtyard. Primavera looks up at the meaty legs and remembers the rhymes, the bleeding bowl of cow's flesh.

The giants smack their lips. One goes up to the cage of faunesses and reaches through the bars, poking at their bare chests. They shiver. One of them, a tall one with dark curls and pink-rimmed eyes, spits and hisses.

"Now, now," says Gunn. "Be good creatures. These are some of my best customers."

One of the giants pokes into the bird-women's cage. Then he sees Primavera hiding. His eyes swirl.

"Little Miss Muffett." He cups his testicles.

Gunn says, "No, sorry. You can't have her.

She's mine. How about this pretty bird? She'll stroke you with her feathers."

The giant pouts, but he does not come nearer to Primavera. What can this man Gunn do that makes even these massive, clotted men obey him? she wonders.

Gunn opens the bird cage and drags Zephyra and two other bird-women out. They hardly struggle. He puts leashes around their necks.

The giants have forgotten her. But Primavera is still shuddering as they lead the creatures out of the courtyard.

Gunn seizes her wrist, stopping the flow of blood there the way he has done at her throat, her waist.

Gunn has not forgotten.

The next day Primavera goes back down to see Zephyra. The bird-women lie crumpled in their cage. Primavera can see new lines in Zephyra's face. The skin under her eyes is dark and dry, pebbley.

Primavera goes up to the cage and puts her hand through the bars. Zephyra reaches out and holds her fingers. Both women are so cold neither notices the ice of the other.

Then Zephyra sees the glint of blue beneath the metal collar, the blue softness brushing against Primavera's breast—River's necklace.

Gunn almost ripped it off the other night, but

then he laughed and said, "So, you're trying to turn into a Mutant now?"

Without taking her eyes off the feathers, Zephyra says, "Where did you get that?"

Primavera tries to answer, but nothing comes out.

"I have a child. I was taken away from him."

Primavera moves closer.

"He is named River."

Primavera's eyes light with the memory of the bird-boy. Of course. Yes. She grasps the necklace.

The bird-woman knows then. "You've seen him. Is he all right?"

Nodding, Primavera imagines her own mother begging a stranger for this same answer. She can see her mother's sorrow in Zephyra's eyes as if Calliope had entered the bird-woman for a moment.

"If you ever escape, go to him. Tell him how I love him. Help him."

Primavera nods again. She looks down in shame. Why did she leave the child? She wants to say, we will escape together, but not only does she have no voice, she has no hope.

She can hardly walk again today.

All she can do is take off River's necklace and press it through the bars into Zephyra's cramped hand.

"Go below," Zephyra says, and Primavera

thinks she means Under. She remembers Arcadie lying by the riverbank, glowing with beauty cream that disguised her death. But then Zephyra says, "In the blue room in the floor beneath the pony-girl is a trap door. It leads to the catacombs under the house. Do not look around you. Walk straight ahead. In the third room is a cage. The horse-man is there. Maybe you can help each other."

What?

Gunn is coming. The women in the cages cower. Primavera sees the vision of the horse's head nailed to the wall.

ZEPHYRA

Silent One who has seen my child, go swiftly into the dark passageways.

When I was alive—for now I am not alive though my heart beats to bursting in my chest when the giants come—when I was alive I had a child. When he was born I thought of the body of water that ran through my dreams—so clear you could see the sparkling pink and jade sand beneath, except where lilies grew. He was tiny and wise. He resembled his father who ran off one night, mad, into the Desert seeking the Garden and was found later dead from thirst. But

River was my child also, with blue feathers growing on his scalp.

We lived in a city of filth and darkness. Stacks of bones and garbage filled the streets. Children wandered through abandoned buildings eating paint peelings off of the walls. We hardly ever went out because the people laughed and pointed and called us devils.

One day we were reading in our home of broken glass when a man came to see us. No one ever ventured into the dead land at the edge of the city where my child and I lived; they feared it was haunted. But this man was not afraid. He told us there was a festival in the town and he wanted us to join in. He said all we had to do was stand on a stage for people to see and he would give us food and gifts. No one would harm us, he said. River backed away, but I thought we should go. River never spoke to anyone but me, though he could have passed for human, and since his father left he hardly ever saw men. This man looked wealthy. I thought that maybe he had come from the Garden that River's father never found. And besides, we were hungry. I picked River up and carried him in my arms, following the man.

We got into the silver truck. It was filled with other creatures like me—women with feathers and women with animal legs. Some still believed they were going to the festival, but others were weeping or screaming. I knew then, as soon as the man shut the doors behind us, that we were lost.

"Where is he taking us?" the women cried.

"Will he kill us?"

River clung to me. I knew I had to find a way to free him.

I whispered to him, "Run through the doors when he opens them again. Run as fast as you can and do not stop until you get home. Hide in a dirt trough. When I can I will come back to you."

He was shaking so much; I was afraid he wouldn't be able to leave me. But when the man opened the door to shove in a small girl with the lower body of a pony, I pushed his shoulders and he almost flew out. He was so small and silent that the man didn't even notice.

That was the last I saw of my child.

The truck was put on a boat and we were taken across the lifeless water surrounding our city, then driven into the Desert.

Finally we stopped and the man chained us together and brought us into his palace. The pony-woman, Rainia, tried to bite him and he led her away. The rest of us were put in these cages.

There were other women-creatures like us here already. They told us about the man who had taken us.

He had come to this place of marble when it

was the home of beautiful, all-human women whom men could sleep with for money. When they saw his body they laughed at him. There was something terribly wrong with him, but no one knew what it was. They only knew that these women laughed and this infuriated the man. He came back one night and killed them all.

"Blood steamed through the catacombs under the house," a fauness told us. "Organs were spilled. It was a massacre."

Then the man decided he wanted to stay in the palace. He cleaned everything up. If anyone came to see the women, he said they had moved away. But he wanted to have a business for himself. He went all over the land looking for "Mutants," as he calls us. He put us in cages and sold our bodies over and over again to the little men who came with things crafted from the iron or gold they had mined or to the ogres with their carcasses of meat. *Sells* our bodies.

He never takes us to his chambers, but every so often he will find an all-human woman and keep her there. And eventually she disappears.

Beware, Silent One.

Go down into the catacombs.

At night in the room all of red, Primavera tries not to think of what the women had seen that had made them laugh. And would make this man pour their blood until the rooms under the house all became as red as this one.

She dreams of the room where she flew with Paul in another dream. Now women with all their limbs hacked off hang from the high ceiling. She can hear a child weeping.

She wakes feeling mutilated, a head and trunk with stumps for arms and legs, wanting her mother, though she can hardly remember even her mother's face.

The next night no giants come to the house. When Gunn is asleep Primavera rises from the bed. She takes her flask of water, although with the collar on her neck she can barely swallow. She takes a candle. She does not wait to put on shoes or a robe but runs down the marble hallway, peering into the many rooms.

Pink room of silk rose canopies.

Black room of crushed velvet and black pearls.

Yellow room of silk crepe streamers and stuffed yellow birds.

Green room of emerald-spark sequin hangings.

Purple room of iris tapestries.

White room of lace and headless death-pale stone torsos.

All are soiled and torn and falling into ruin. All are haunted. None are blue.

And then, finally, she comes to it. The blue is

like the flashes in the night sky before the rain comes to her almost-forgotten paradise. It seems about to crackle. It seems to illuminate itself from within. Three walls are covered with bunchy blue satin. The fourth is floor to ceiling books, all bound in the same electric blue leather. The floor is a blue stone like lapis lazuli. There is a satin bed with a shell-shaped headboard. The tremulous wave patterns of candlelight on the blue walls and floor and bed make Primavera feel she is deep beneath a dream-sea.

In the corner of the room stands the pony-girl. She has a young woman's face and upper body and the lower body of a small, sturdy, dappled horse. Her eyes are glass and there are crude stitch marks on her rough skin. She is smiling as if her lips have been pinned.

Primavera lifts her carefully aside, trying not to look too closely. The pony-girl feels cold and scratchy, heavy. Primavera falls to her knees and thinks too late of the bruises that the man may find there later from bone against stone. Her hands scramble like small animals, hardly a part of her, seeking the opening.

Suddenly the floor gives way and she almost falls down the stone staircase that is revealed. An ancient stench of damp and decay blasts up at her. The revulsion she feels is nothing like that of returning to the bed in the red room, so she goes down, drawing the trap door closed over her head.

The stone stairs wind farther and farther and her candle, quivering, ready to go out, is her only guide. She thinks of going Under with Arcadie and is thankful that the tunnel leading down there stole the memory of itself. This place does not offer that gift.

Finally the passageway. She stumbles over something, cutting her bare foot, and lowers her candle to see what litters the floor. Everywhere are bones. She tries not to think of the women who once danced and made love and languished above in the marble rooms. These are only lifeless substance—like stone—she tells herself. There is no blood here except her own from the small, fresh cut. No cries of horror but her own stifled ones.

Only the stench, and she can breathe through her mouth, although somehow the smell reaches her that way, seeping into her gums and tongue and down her throat.

The tiny rooms branching off of the passageway contain nothing but darkness, she tells herself. Except for the one room she seeks. What is there?

She sees the cage and the dark shape bent inside it, the almost phosphorescent glow of two eyes watching her. She moves closer despite the impulse to run away.

He is huddled behind the bars, his head

against iron. She comes nearer still and the huge animal haunches shift, crumple beneath him, all that withering power. The rippled muscles, the whiteness of them so close to the surface, not hidden by fat or much flesh and the way at the groin horseness becomes the slim man-hips. The beating of pulse must be there, she thinks, something so vulnerable, that junction, the strangeness of his skin which is, all over—even at the torso, arms, neck, face—a thick white, a sheen as of sleek animal flesh, but finer so it is more human than horse flesh where it covers the bulk of animal haunch and the four surprisingly slender legs. His eyes are deep brown but strangely light filled, the wide orb of horse's eyes, the heavy lid with long but far-apart lashes. They almost look lined with brown pencil. A broad nose, softly full lips. When he parts them—large strong teeth.

"Who are you?" he mumbles. His lips are cracked, ridged with dryness, papery; they would tear, she thinks, if she touched them.

She tries to speak, her hands at her throat.

"That's all right." He pauses. "I am called Horse."

She gives him her flask of water, pressing it between the bars and he reaches his hand out. The knuckles are big and dirt-caked. She sees the tremor in his fingertips as he grasps the flask.

He drinks, gulping it all down, thrusting back his head, exposing the ripples of his throat.

"Can you tell me your name?"

She moves her hands wildly, a mad woman.

"You have to leave," he says. "I am afraid he will find you here." His eyes shine. When he gives back the empty flask their hands touch. Then, through the bars, he reaches up and presses his fingers lightly against the hollow of her neck, that place fibrous with hurt.

The touch throbs in her as she runs back through the passageway, gasping for breath, up the stairs, up into the blue room where she sets the pony-girl back in place.

She tries to keep that touch later as the man stuffs the cold fist of himself into her body. At least it is dark; he will not see her bruised knees or the transformation that has occurred in her.

It is the memory of Horse's eyes that makes it possible for her finally to sleep each night. The pain in her throat is gone. She feels as if she has swallowed a soothing elixir.

She dreams of Horse. He is galloping through a house full of children. In each room, for each child, he lights a small lamp. The lamps are shaped like stars, planets, fireflies, tiny winged people.

She cannot stop thinking of the horse-man. She is afraid to go back to him, though.

At last she is able to see Zephyra again without Gunn knowing.

"Did you find him?"

Primavera does not have to even nod her head. Zephyra sees it.

"Did he touch you?"

Primavera looks puzzled.

"He is a great healer."

Primavera's hand goes to her throat where, despite the strangling collar, the lumps of pain seem to have melted.

"Perhaps you can speak now? Try to say your name."

Primavera stares at Zephyra. She has become so crippled that even the possibility of her own voice seems unreal.

"Try."

She opens her mouth. Out of the tunnel of her throat emerges something, some creature, mutilated, broken but still alive.

"Primavera," Primavera says.

"Do not let the man know," Zephyra whispers. "Keep silent. But return to the catacombs when you can."

Before Primavera can test her voice to see if she can sing, she hears Gunn's boots.

The horse-man's cheekbones cut the dark. His hair is starry silver and his hands are beautiful with the almost rectangular fingertips, the strong veins. Hands still like sculpture holding the bars.

"Thank you," she says to him.

He smiles and she fears for his delicate dry lips, but the smile makes him even more beautiful. "You speak now."

"I am Primavera."

"Spring."

"Yes. Thank you for helping me."

"I wish I could do more for you. Does he hurt you very badly?"

She cannot use the voice that has been returned to her to answer this. She looks down.

Horse grips the bars of his cage with his fists. He shows his teeth and throws back his head. "I would kill him. I would kill him. I would kill him."

"Tell me about yourself," she says, trying to calm him, lulling herself with the sound of her voice.

"You should get back upstairs. He may find out."

"Tell me quickly. I need something to think of when he hurts me. I want to know you."

"Not now. He may come."

"I will come back to you," she says.

Gunn is sitting at his long gold and glass table eating the rare meat that the giants have brought. Primavera can hear him from the courtyard. Sometimes he makes her sit with him and she can feel the tearing of the flesh as if it were her own. Tonight he has allowed her to leave dinner early. She has promised him mutely with bowed head and clasped hands that she will go upstairs and prepare the bed.

First, though, she will go to Zephyra. She must move quietly—a shadow.

She can almost see the bird-woman's nerves wincing. "You are in pain. What can I do?" she whispers.

"Have you seen the horse-man again?"

"Yes. He told me not to."

"He wants to protect you. But I believe you can still both help each other."

"I will try to go back there." Then: "What is it like to be a mother?"

"Why do you ask?"

"I think of her—my mother. I see you mourning without River."

"It is very painful sometimes. It is painful to love that much. And yet when I think of River hatching—all damp and dreamy—there is nothing that made me feel closer to . . . "

"To what?"

"I have no name for it. Spirit. Stars. Eternity. And for a woman to give birth right from her body without the separation of the egg's hard shell. That must be truly sublime. It might be even harder for that woman to give up her child."

Zephyra looks knowingly at Primavera. "She is waiting for you," Zephyra says. "She has not given up."

"Does she know I love her?"

"She knows. Go now. And find him again soon. He will help you return to her."

HORSE

I was born in the circus. My father Flint had been captured by them as a boy and brought to the city of pleasures called Elysia. He was so young that he did not think of escape; the circus tent and the wagon he slept in were all that were needed to keep him caged. His muscles grew weak and sore. He ran around the tent all day trying to feel the power that he sensed was his, but he never found it. His mind ached in this cramped world. He wanted to read, to learn, to know, but they spoke to him as if he had the mind of an animal and not just an animal's legs. Sometimes he felt a lust that he thought must only belong to the horse part of him. It was ferocious and painful, but he had nowhere to direct it except into his own hands in the dark, leaving him shuddering and even weaker. The circus women frightened him. He imagined them screaming in horror if he approached them. Or, later, screaming in pain trying to deliver a monster child with hooves—a child that should never have invaded their wombs.

Then they brought my mother to him. Her name was Amulet. She had white flesh and hair like diamond dust and pale blue eyes. And she had a woman's torso sloping into the body of a horse. She knew how to read and write. Together they stole books and she taught him by candle-light in their tent. He remembered suddenly how it had felt to run with his mother in the starlit fields, breathing the dark dreams of flowers, his hooves trampling the earth and the dew covering the more delicate skin of his arms and chest with a glistening netting. He leaned his head against my mother's loins and wept. They must have loved each other fiercely then, the only familiar creature in a city of strangers, the only other hoofed-one with human brain and hands that they now knew. Their hearts were also the same, but neither could have said if they had the heart of man or beast. Maybe their hearts were differ-ent, and mine also. They did not try to escape. By then my father had resigned himself to his life. Elysia seemed to have that effect. Even on the ones who did not get to enjoy its baubles and trinkets. It seemed to cast a lulling spell. My mother might have begged my father some-times—I seem to remember it vaguely, she weeping on the other side of our wagon, "Please let's leave here. We can run and find those fields

where we were born. Maybe even our parents."
He hushing her, "Amulet, you'll wake him. Our
parents are gone by now. Maybe those fields are
gone, too. And I can't run fast anymore. We must
try to be content with what we have been given.
We have a son now."

So my mother gave in and we stayed. We per-
formed in the circus, running around and around
the ring, sometimes with one of them on our
backs. There was a beautiful young girl who
would ride me sometimes. She was different; she
had a narrow wolfish face, wild hair, and warm
slender thighs with long sculpted muscles.
When she gripped onto me I reared in the air
and tears startled my eyes, but she never
whipped me. She clung on and rode me around
the tent. Her silky dress brushed my flanks and
our sweat ran together, pooling in the hollow of
my back—she never used a saddle. At night
sometimes I would come to her. I was afraid I
was too large, but she told me to love her. "You
aren't frightened of me?" I would whisper, and
she would kiss my mouth to silence. She was
how I found strength to run in my little circle
every day, to bow my head before them. She
brought me a book about people who fell in love
and were transformed into rivers and trees. Some
were part animal. She said that at one time in
another world I would have been thought of like
a god.

That was before the man came. I do not know what he did to my parents or to the other creatures of the circus—those of us who were not all human. The Mutants. I was spared death. But what I have been given instead is much worse.

The man calls me Horse.

But I can remember my father massaging his lower back where it met the animal part, the fatigue in his eyes; I can remember my mother, Amulet, cradling my head against her breast, whispering in her gentle throaty voice of endless open fields. I can remember the feral face of the girl, Arcadie. I can remember my name, the one my parents gave to me, seeing how I burned with the wildness they feared and treasured in their own blood. It is a strange name that speaks of death, but they must have needed some way to cry out.

My real name is Pyre.

"Pyre."

He has told Primavera his name. He has told her about his love, the girl who looks like her. His voice sounds weak, but his eyes are still filled with their eerie, somehow comforting, light.

She thinks of the night-lights in her dream.

"Arcadie," she says. "I know her. I knew . . . "

His hooves rake the floor of the cage. "You know her. Is she all right?"

She wishes the voice he has given back to her could tell him what he wishes to hear, and that it were true.

"No. She must be all right. I'm the one that should be dead if one of us should be dead." He knows without the words.

"She loved you so much," is all Primavera can think to say. She hears Zephyra telling her, "If you ever see River again tell him I love him." She knows Arcadie would have wished the same words told to her lover. Now it sounds like nothing.

Pyre bows his head. "Go now," he says. "I don't want him to find you here. You must not come again. He would kill you if he knew."

She wants to feed him apples and honey and take him to see the sunrise. She wants to swim with him in misty blue water that heals him the way he healed her voice. She wants to bask in him, hold onto him. She wants them to make each other better, all better.

Yearning is not grief, she thinks. Before Pyre she thought it was, but it is not. Yearning is a beautiful youth with a wound-mouth and fine fingers. Yearning believes in something. Yearning still has strong legs and a mouth that remembers how to sing or at least can imagine.

Paul once sang inside of her like the blue shadows at twilight in the Desert. And he was some paradise—flowers and palm trees, music.

Yearning is the muse. But grief withers in the cage, the color of smoke, and even the muse cannot save him.

She dreams that she is looking into a mirror. Instead of her own face she sees the horse-man. She is in his eyes. He is crying.

"Don't cry," she says. "The little dolls will get wet."

"But *you* are crying."

"Yes. I miss my family. Are they all right?"

Pyre disappears. In the mirror now—Calliope and Dionisio. Just for a moment. They are holding their arms out to her. She looks into their eyes, trying to see four tiny Primaveras.

Her parents' eyes are empty.

"Did he kill her?" Pyre asks.

She has come down to see him again. She cannot stay away from him. He is pacing in his cage, gripping and releasing the bars.

"No. She died from a kind of overdose."

"He killed her. If he hadn't taken me away it would not have happened."

"Why did he take you?"

"He thinks we are imperfect."

"But the rest are all women."

"And me. Sometimes he just comes down here and watches. Sometimes he ties me up and does things to me. Now he mostly sends scraps of garbage down a chute to keep me alive—barely."

She wants to release him, open the cage; they would run together. She would ride him, swept in a pink-lit wind and a fall of dawn-soaked flowers; he would feel the earth beneath those hooves that here, locked up, will chip and shatter like brittle shells or glass.

At least she must sing for him. She has been afraid to try before. Now she opens her throat.

No song comes out. He has healed her speaking voice, but still she cannot sing.

He thrashes his head back and forth and she can do nothing.

"Speak to me," he says. "Tell me something."

Primavera tells Pyre about the place that was once a desert and became a garden, the ravine that was once dry and then ran with healing waters. She tells him about the music her family played, how it bound them together and transformed whatever it touched. "They called themselves Ecstasia."

She speaks of Rafe, who was the first to venture away from Elysia with only his drum. For the first time she thinks of how brave her mother's brother must have been to pull himself away from the spell of the city. He is like her, she realizes, although their journeys were reversed— she moving toward the artifice and he away. But

Rafe also sought change and an escape from his obsessions.

Primavera talks about Paul, too. She tells Pyre that Paul sang with her when she was a child and that he loves Rafe. "Paul is the main reason I left," she says. She does not have to say much more. Pyre's eyes are aglow. It is as if he can see Paul standing there with them—tall, angular, haloed—as if he can hear the rough and celestial, bitter and mellifluous voice.

"My father's name is Dionisio," Primavera says. "For years now I haven't felt close to him. I judged him for his softness. But now I see how kind he is. He loved me more when I was a little child, but maybe that is because I only let him love me then." Thinking of Dionisio now, Primavera remembers how safe she once felt in his arms. She remembers him pretending to be a rabbit, a monkey, a dog, and a lion to make her laugh. Hopping, screeching, barking, roaring Dionisio—a menagerie. He would let her tug his floppy curls and pull him along with her anywhere. He would cry when she sang, pretending that he wasn't. *Don't cry, Papa. Mama, Papa is tanged with tears.* She remembers when she decided she would no longer say Mama and Papa. She was about ten. If she slipped she would pinch herself. She wanted to sound like a grownup. "Why don't you call me Papa anymore?" he asked her.

"And your mother?" Pyre asks.

"Calliope." The name is the closest thing to a song Primavera has uttered within these walls.

"Tell me."

"She is my best friend. She knows my thoughts. She is the most beautiful woman I have ever seen and the kindest. I have hurt her by leaving."

"She will understand," Pyre says.

They look at each other. Primavera finds it hard to breathe.

"Gunn will be up soon," she says.

"Go now."

The pony-girl has been moved aside. The trap door opened. Primavera has gone down the stairs. Pyre is there, just beyond.

"What are you doing here?" Gunn says.

She feels as if a fist has been jammed down her throat to her heart. A scream almost—but then she remembers. Do not let him know that she has her voice. She staggers backwards, dropping her candle. The flame sputters and dies.

He takes her shoulders in his cold hands. She can hear his feet kicking aside bones in the darkness, the bones scratching like claws.

"You must never come down here again. I will slaughter you like the rest of them. I will flay your skin and wear it as a cloak. I will make a mask from the skin of your inner thigh." He says it quietly, without emotion. She can see his face in the darkness, maggot-white.

"You need me," he says.

She can only stare mutely.

Do not go to Pyre. Punish me but forget Pyre.

"You need me. I am what you were looking for. What you wanted to become. You hate the woman you are. You hate your song. You hate your flowers. You hate your mother and father for trying to entrap you. You think I keep you locked up? They kept you locked up. You hate the pretty man who didn't desire you and the pretty man he desired. You hate yourself. So you came to me. Do you know why? You wanted to learn who you could be. My power is clean and hard and erect as hate. I am all you have always wanted to become."

Be silent, Pyre. Do not make a sound.

Gunn does not go to Pyre. Instead, he wrenches her arm, pulling her back up to his room. "You are becoming me now," he whispers. "I have given you everything you have ever wanted."

Pyre is lying in the corner of the cage and does not stir when he sees her.

"What is it?" she asks him.

She wishes she could sing for him. She cannot even fill his cage with a profusion of sweet-white gardenia cakes and red-wine roses. But even then, what good is the gift of making flowers bloom? she thinks. What does it mean? That would not save him.

"There was a lady in here before," he mumbles, stretching out his hand to the bars. His pupils are hardly visible, his eyes flat and dark, staring into air. "She looked like a fairy. Did you see her?"

"No, Pyre. Come back. There isn't a fairy here."

"Oh, yes. Yes, there is. You'll see. The fairy. If you see the water fairy, then you die."

"Pyre. Stay here. What happened?"

She would sing for him armloads of silver-flecked irises.

"Primavera."

She peers into the dark cage. There is something wet gleaming on the floor.

"He hurt you." She feels a surge of pain in her throat.

"You must stop coming here," says Pyre, his voice suddenly clear. "You must not. He will kill both of us."

She dreams of Pyre.

She is in a field of tree-tall flowers; she is wearing wreaths and wraps, cascades and braids of flowers. A flood of light polishes the earth.

She finds the horse-man sleeping in green and violet shade. His face is peaceful, his brow smooth. She kneels beside him. They are caught in a cyclone of butterflies. When the winged creatures disperse, leaving her covered in pollen, she kisses Pyre's lips. They taste of the water of the Sound—cold with an essence of clear sweetness.

Pyre opens his eyes.

"Spring," he says.

PYRE

Spring.

Are you the water fairy?

Among the rushes she is translucent green and silver, calling my name in a thin strangled voice. We meet death much more easily than life. The struggle and contortions of the womb, the scream. For most of us death is no such battle. The womb is worth fighting for, but not this life. Not for me.

Except you. But are you life or my sweet death, promising freedom from this pain? Death dressed in white and shackles, you came down mute, bringing me water. Your skin is cold and your face has an unearthly beauty. You are like Arcadie's ghost.

And you are also the goddess of the spring. The hurt has made you pale, ethereal, but sometimes I see the glow of living blossoms reflected in dark eyes. I see the singing child in the woman who can now just barely speak.

I tell you not to return for fear he will find out. But I want you to touch me. If you bring sweet death. If you bring me resurrection, Primavera.

CALLIOPE

I want to wander out into the night and find you. An ancient crone seeking, in the body of her daughter, the magic potion to make her alive and young again.

When I do go wandering, your father and Paul and Rafe bring me back. "She will return," they say, pouring their love into me like a healing potion to keep the dark visions away. But I remember what the boat man said. I remember your songs in the river.

Sometimes I wish I had kept you in a gilded cage like a little bird. You would have been safe there.

I know a tale of a princess whose mother put her daughter's soul into the body of a little bird. The princess was safe as long as her mother kept the bird safe. The cage was guarded by magic trees and monsters.

But you could not be kept in any cage. No matter what danger there was, you wanted to face it. I did not want to be the monster who imprisoned your soul, pretending that I was keeping you from harm when I was keeping you from life.

Last night as I was walking by the caves I heard the trickle of Sound water speak to me. It said, "Do as you would want her to do."

"But what about the demons of Hunger and Disease and War?" I cried, falling to my knees on the bank.

"Do as you would want her to do."

I would not want you to go running out into the night weeping.

I would want you to sing, Primavera. That is all I want. For then you would be safe and loved and free.

So I must cut down the magic trees and release the ogres and open the gold cage of my heart and set free your spirit. I must play my music. Every song of love is yours.

If only you can still sing.

PAUL

Primavera.

Under, I cursed you for leaving us. I hated you for taking life away from us. But it was your life you were taking back and making your own. No matter what the risk, this is what you had to do. Like when I left home and Paradisia because I felt I would have withered up without the touch of men. Or like when I left Elysia to find Rafe. No one could have told me to do anything different. They could have said, you won't accept or love yourself any more than now; the skin on your face will swell and burn and weep. They could have said, one day you and Rafe will no longer hold each other in the night. You will have gardens, but then you will watch them turn again to dust. The child you so adore will disappear and the river of your voice will dry up. Would I not have gone on either of these journeys? Of course I would have gone.

Forgive me for my hateful words beneath the earth. Know that not only did I love you as my daughter and my friend and an enchantress of song, but that, if things in this life had been different, I would have loved you as you loved me.

I think sometimes that we were lovers in another life like you said in your song. I pretended I didn't know who those words were for, but I think you were the man then and I was the woman. That explains the lightness I feel in me, the empty space in me awaiting a man's fullness. And you who are as strong beneath your veils and slight limbs as any warrior. It explains also this secret and tormenting familiarity and this forbidden desire which again and again I must learn to forget and to release. The lesson of this life is not for me to touch you again. It is to give you up to your new self and to watch over you with the wisdom of ancient memory; it is to accept who I am now and not feel shame about the spirit that my male body contains, the spirit who calls relentlessly out for another man, with a cry more powerful than even my wanting you.

I don't know if this means anything now. If you return I won't love you as a lover, but I will be kinder to you and more clear with you as I should have been before.

I don't even know if you are alive.

The Desert is a true desert once again. Ecstasia lies fallow. Whatever sunshine, fertile flowering earth, clear water, radiant air we might have known is gone. We will accept this. We came to the Desert expecting nothing more. Those years with you were a great gift.

We can accept a parched old age. But only let us know that you still live, bringing the flowersong of your beauty to someone somewhere, Primavera.

RAFE

Since I cannot grow one, I try to build a garden.

I collect rocks and chip away at them, stacking them up to look like plants. But they are more like angry stone men ready to topple over.

Still, this is the closest thing to a garden I can make.

I began this garden of stone while Paul was away. I wanted to give him something when he came back. I told him, "We can call it Primavera's Garden." It was my way of asking his forgiveness for the things I said about my sister's daughter.

Sometimes at night when I can't sleep I walk out here and look at the stone garden in the moonlight. The rocks cast shadows on the sand when the moon is full—rows of judges with long slabs of cheek and hard-cut, prying noses. They seems to be saying, "Rafe, remember what you said about Primavera? Remember how you made Paul suffer?"

They are nothing like flowers.

I remember how I first came to the Desert. You know, I didn't hate the barren world of sand and rock then. It soothed and purified me in a way. It was a way to rid my body of the sweet poisons of Elysia.

Now I've become used to an abundantly green place so the thought of desert frightens me. But there are many worse things. There could be life without my loved ones Under; that can't even be called life. Being here together is life. We would be all right out here except for the fact that Primavera is gone.

So I build this garden for her.

Paul didn't take me in his arms. He didn't sing a song about it. He just said, "Thank you, Rafer." He looked so pale after his journey.

I felt helpless. I went and stacked some more stones on top of each other, hoping they would not fall over.

One night soon we'll all come out here and play music in Primavera's Garden. And then maybe she will hear the song wherever she is and somehow it will help her return to us.

DIONISIO

Did we sacrifice our daughter? Make her sing for us and we'll have paradise for awhile.

But at the same time we wanted other things. We gave up Elysia and we thought we got a better bargain out here, but maybe we all still wanted the riches and the sweets. Maybe she sensed that and went looking for it for us. Inside maybe we thought that somehow we could have it all.

It's too much for anyone, especially one young girl. Did we sell her soul to give us what we wanted? Now is she living out our desire?

She is like a fruit tree. We watered her with love but we plucked all her branches. We took too much. Maybe she dreamed of being a silver tree with chips of glass for leaves so that no one could take from her and she wouldn't want anything. The wanting is the hardest.

I want to be a father. I never had a father and maybe it's too late now. If she never comes back it is too late. I want to be her father and guide her. Not just let her feed us with her beauty and her songs but make her feel respect and listen to the dark spirit in her.

My bass lies silent in my lap like a dead child.

Don't we think we can do anything for ourselves anymore? We're her family. We can help her. Just listen to the silence; it contains within it all the music that will heal us. It's just been so long we think we've forgotten how to hear it.

ECSTASIA'S SONG

There was no more water and there was no
   green
When our fairy daughter went on her
   journey
And there were no flowers, all the gardens
   died
When our guiding spirit went out on her
   ride
I tell you now I wanted somehow
To return us to a world
Before pain and sorrow
Cut through gardens like a sword

And I want the love to take us
To a different kind of life
Still we must learn the lesson
How to grieve and how to cry
I tell you now I wanted somehow
For the carnivals to die
We watch the withering destruction
And we wait here for the bride

"I am what you wanted to become," Gunn says. He is taking off his clothes. The very air in the room changes as his body is revealed, clammy and chill as a corpse. In the darkness she can see gleaming the sharpened metal piece between his legs.

"They laughed at me," he says. "But look what I have now. I will use this on you the next time."

She thinks, Pyre. Flint struck against Amulet and the fire flared. Flint struck Amulet and the fire flared. That was life-making lovemaking. Not this. Not his.

She thinks, Pyre, I will remember how, when I came down, you turned your head and gazed, eyes so dark with extinguished circuses and wasted blasted meadows never seen but once dreamed. Your ancient eyes were the underworld but the Under from where all life is reborn. I will also remember you young in sleep—the colt that sometimes twitched his limbs within your limbs, the long-lashed trembling-footed colt whose forehead was so smooth, a warm little star hollow thumb print between the eyes. The same—just smaller—as that place on your chest, that indentation near your heart. Pyre, I could kill him for what he has done to you. I want to drink your tears and take you inside of me to then become a creature who is both of us together. I am ready now. There is no more time to be afraid.

"You must not come here."

She reaches her hands out to him. He unfolds, stumbling to his feet, and lumbers toward her. In the candlelight his skin has a grayish tint. He leans his head against the bars. She puts her fingers into his hair and feels the pulse of life at the roots. Her hands tingle.

"I used to sing," she whispers. "I could make flowers grow. If I still could, I would sing you a field, paradise."

Suddenly he presses his bare chest to the bars. Straining to be free. His face looks as if he is being lashed.

"I hated the flowers," she says. "I felt they were too much. I hated my love and desire."

"You are flowers and love and desire," says Pyre. "You are spring."

"Now I know. Now I have seen the man and I know what I could become without the flowers and the songs. But I have no songs left."

"And I have no healing left. Forgive me."

"No. That's not why I came here again. I wanted to see you one more time. I know I can't keep coming back—he would destroy us both—but I wanted to tell you that I would give you every song I have ever made if I could."

Pyre says, "I dream of holding you."

She moves closer. She puts her hands through the bars and touches his bare chest. The skin is surprisingly warm. She can feel his whole chest vibrate with his heartbeat. With one finger she traces the line down the center of his abdomen, the sections as defined as mosaic tile.

"You are a great beauty," he says. "I am a monster. He tells me that." He lowers his head. She remembers a white horse pressing the warm velvet of his nose into her palm.

"He is a monster. Pyre. Pyre." The desire makes her voice ache.

Between the iron bars Pyre and Primavera's lips press, his still full but paper-thin, hers like forgotten petals drained of color now. She can feel the pressure of his teeth like anguish beneath the tenderness of lips. She can feel the howls in both their throats. Her hand claws against his chest. He grabs the fingers, twisting them into his fist.

My heart, she thinks, is a plot of earth. His kiss reaching down into me, planting. Out of my heart will grow such blossoms as we have never

seen before. They will rise up like warriors. From
their centers will spring a world.

Their whole bodies are pressed together now,
but instead of solid flesh they feel the division of
the bars. She swoons like a strange white flower,
dropping to her knees before him.

"Sing," he whispers. "Sing Primavera."

She bows her head against his groin. Then she
looks up.

down beneath this cage there are green crystal
caves where a violet
river runs
I know this
when you touched me
then I heard it
felt its cool coursing through the dead iron
   bars

let us put our ears to the stone bone floor
and listen to the river
I tell you not everyone can hear it

on the bank we will sit eating over-sweet
   summer melon
the leaf eyes peering through green
the brown limbs quick through branches

I will give you an amber eye ring
with a wine fire inside
I will give you a serpent necklace

full of transparent waves
a veil made of wind
and a wreath of lemon blossoms

you will put your heavy head in my lap
and hear the song of my blood

there are pools filled with violets greens in us
deep reaches of shells and water plants
the inner light
of crystalline fish
that heal us heal us
places where the salt does not even sting
  the wound in my throat
or your chest
but soothes
I tell you even now I hear those waters
  sometimes
though I feel hollow
do you hear them?

And as Primavera sings, it is as if four musicians, very far away in a garden of stone flowers, are playing with her. A thin dark-haired man whom she resembles makes the drums pulse as if they are filled with blood. A tall golden man makes his guitar shine like a magical night-light when he touches the strings. Another man lets himself weep as he plays his bass, his tears falling onto the vines that seem to grow from inside the instrument. And a woman's hands on the keyboards guide Primavera's song as the woman's love once guided what was not yet Primavera to become Primavera in the womb, as the woman's body once guided her daughter into the world.

Primavera can feel all of them in her heart. She wonders if Pyre hears them, too.

The song floats through the catacombs and up the stairs and out the trap door and into the blue room where the pony-girl stands. It floats past the white room, the purple room, the green room, the yellow room, the black room, the pink room. As it passes the red room, Gunn stirs in his sleep. But before he can get up and go into the courtyard the song has arrived there.

The bird-women and the faunesses and the mermaids hear it. The bird-women raise their skeletal wings. The faunesses stamp their brittle hooves. The mermaids swim in maddened circles, chasing their tails, and rear their heads out of the water. And the silence is broken.

All together the voices join in. Voices scarred. Voices resonant. The scream of birds. The raw cough of goats. The gurgle of fish. The birth cries and love cries and death cries of women. The cage bars shake as if they are made of reeds.

Gunn cannot stop what happens. And what is it that happens? Below in the catacombs, Primavera watches as Pyre's cage becomes an enchanted forest. From among the succulent green vines thick as arms, thick as the bars of a cage, from among the labial lilies and the phallic orchids, steps the horse-man. He seems to have grown in size; his muscles expanding with power. The torment is gone from his face. Primavera thinks, it is as if he has bathed in the Sound. His lips are moist, healed.

He places his hands on her neck and the metal collar dissolves into a wreath of light petals, wet with nectar.

He places his hands on her waist and, swiveling around, he lifts her onto his white horseback. Their bodies are touching now, thigh to ribs, breast to back. Her skin feels hot and cold at once, wet against his soothing hard dryness. She thinks, he is my other limbs lost.

He runs over the bone-paved floor to the staircase and takes the path of Primavera's song. She sings on and on until her song and the song of the women join together in the courtyard.

Gunn is hypnotized by it. He does not stop to arm himself. He is drawn helplessly forward.

But when he sees what is happening, Gunn wakes from the spell. He heaves a stone from the glass garden against the tank where the mermaids live. The tank shatters, water spurting out like blood from a wound. Shards of glass burst upwards in a fountain. And the mermaids fall out onto the stone floor in a gasping heap, their tails making a thick, wet, smacking sound.

Gunn takes another stone, stoops down and begins pounding the mermaids' frail skulls against the courtyard floor as if he is crushing shells. Their greenish weeping-river hair turns red. He exposes the flashing metal between his legs.

The fauness and bird-women's songs turns to a shriek of grief. It is still a song.

The bars of the cages are transforming into thick vines and stalks bearing wide-mouthed blossoms and other flowers shaped like breasts and sex. The bars of the cage are becoming plants or the plants are tearing the bars of the cages apart. The faun-women and the bird-women are stepping shakily out into a sudden wilderness of their own making.

The women descend upon Gunn as the last mermaid's skull shatters. The fury of the caged explodes.

As Pyre and Primavera enter they cannot see Gunn. They only see the wings of the bird-women raised like banners, the bare sinewy backs of the faun-women. They hear the hollow screams. The women seem to be wrenching the man apart—the way he tore his meat at the dinner table—so that they can find if there is any soul in him.

They find nothing of the kind.

5. THE DESERT

We have built a fire for the mermaids. The flames looked like red waves through my tears. Perhaps the fish-women's spirits swam there.

We have buried the dismembered parts of a man's body in the dunes of sand.

We will leave the motorcycle with the horse's head to rust. We will leave the marble palace.

"Join us in the Desert," I say, but the women have other plans. The hoofed women draw veils made from bed canopies over their mouths and run off across the sand. The bird-women ascend into the gray sky with sacks full of the mermaids' ashes to sprinkle over the sea. They are all seeking home.

Pyre stands outside the gates of the palace with his eyes closed and his face turned up to the sky. Rivulets of tainted rain trickle down his brow, down his bare shoulders and chest. Drops form on his horse haunches, gather and tremble before they spill.

I swing my legs over his back.

He is my other limbs lost.

"Do you have the strength?" I ask him, pressing my face against his neck.

"Since you touched me."

I can feel the strength in him the way I could sense water under the earth in the trees and flowers when I was home. It rushes beneath the surface, reverberating currents.

Zephyra's legs move stiffly but her blue eyes are alive. "I am going to find River," she says.

"Do you want us to go with you?" I ask, kneading Pyre's warm shoulder. I cannot stop touching him, marvelling that this form made of energy contains who he is.

"Would you?"

"Of course," says Pyre. "I can carry you both—all three when we get him."

"I will fly beside you," she says. "I may be slow, but I need to try again."

She lifts her face to the sky the way Pyre did. The rain flattens her thin hair against her temples. "River," she whispers. Stirred by the love song of the boy's name, her long-caged wings begin to open like fragile fans of bone and feather.

Zephyra rises. Not high or quickly, but she is

flying. I feel the desire to fall to my knees beneath her shadow.

I can feel Pyre's body gather power. I press my legs against his flanks. I grasp his hips, that place where horse and man are joined.

We ride out into the desert beneath Zephyra's wings, leaving the buried corpse of the man behind.

In Neverland, Pyre and I wait on the shore while Zephyra flies across the water. The gesture of her wings, so sharp and sure, taking her to River, makes me think of my mother.

Calliope is sitting in the lifeless garden where no new blossoms have unfolded. She is not weeping. She is saying, "Daughter, if you still live, find what you must find, whom you must find." My mother is playing her music. She has begun to play again. She is not running after me or trying to invade my thoughts, but her love is flying, always flying, over the oceans, through the deserts, down the cobbled streets, into the palaces, deep into the catacombs of bones and death.

Pyre and I gaze at the bruised sky, the body of water like an oozing cut, the vast dead land spreading around us.

He says, "I've only known the circus of Elysia and then that place."

"I wish you could have stepped outside into paradise."

He torques his neck to look at me with the glowing eyes. I feel the rush of healing again as if he has kissed me. "I have," he says.

my fire
you were not in the desert

there was a dead blue water nymph
you were not beside the ocean

not in the shop windows
though they blazed it was electric

not on the stone portico

you were not in the glass garden

the membranes were tight and dry
I was cold bones today
my skin felt raw
you were nowhere

I dreamed the stinking carcass
death waiting for the pure flame

I dreamed a horse of dirt and twigs
it had a sealed mouth and eyes

then I dreamed that hidden
among the cloven hooves of cliffs

I found a patch of white gem ice
a tree growing out of the ice
and covered with huge fleshy ice-white
    flowers
the air like fruit ices

I knew the vision was within me
and you came

with the camp fire of your limbs you melted
    ice
and the water ran

now we follow that river
traveling home over the blue hills of twilight
we are falling silent into the blue water

color hills of twilight

When Zephyra returns, Pyre and I awaken from the dream of the song. Zephyra lands in the mud beside us. I do not see her child.

"Zephyra?" I am afraid to know.

But she unfolds her wings and there, on her back, tucked into the nest of feathers is River. He clings to her neck, unwilling to let go even for an instant.

I kneel and look into his eyes.

"Fairy," he whispers.

"How are you, River?"

He nods gravely.

"I'm sorry I left you."

"It's all right. You found Mama for me."
"And now we are all going home."

PAUL

I see a figure or a group emerging through
the colorless field among Rafe's stone flowers. I
cannot tell how many. Maybe it is just one person, a strange and beautiful beast with the
lower body of a horse, two torsos—man and
woman—and a pair of wings. Then I see that
the woman is riding the horse-man and that the
wings belong to a third figure who flies just
above them, near enough to seem a part of
them. Finally I see the tiny boy on the back of
the winged woman.

I am aware of the heat of sun breaking
through the clouds, warming the hollow chill in
my lower back that I had thought would be there
forever. The breeze in my hair is like a hundred
stroking hands. I can hear the water of the
Sound bubble into song. The earth seems to stir
with the promise of flowers—enchanted
princesses long asleep.

Primavera is returning.

Before I can call their names, the rest of our
family is running to join me. Calliope gets here
first. Her hands are covered with earth from try-

ing to plant in the hard ground and dried leaves are tangled in her hair.

"Is it real?" she whispers.

"Yes, Callie. She's here," Dionisio says.

I feel Rafe's hand on my shoulder. I look at him and see the young boy who I first fell in love with, the speed-child who I always feared would break the skins of his drums. I see the lithe hero who led the Old Ones up from Under. And I see the sun-lined, still-slender man who has mourned with me all these days the loss of our Spring. He had stopped touching me. He is touching me again. The feeling between us like a concert of all the songs we have ever played.

"Who's that with her?" Dionisio squints at them a little mistrustfully.

But I know it is all right because Calliope is smiling. Her arms are open.

"Fire, Water, and Air," she says as she goes forward to greet her daughter.

PRIMAVERA

This is the wedding day.

In the rose-colored tent my mother dresses me in flowers. My body is draped with garlands, nothing else, and I feel the petals smooth and tender as flesh against my flesh, warm as if they have blood coursing through their thin, thin veins.

My mother adjusts the wreath on my head. She is wearing a purple robe and lilacs in her hair. I see how she has aged, even in the time I have been away, lines cutting her face so deeply that they look almost painful.

"I'm sorry," I say.

"Sorry?" She sits beside me. "Why sorry? This is a day of joy."

"For leaving you and hurting you."

"You had to go." She has not asked me about my journey. Either she has already seen or does not want to know. "You can't be responsible for all of us here. We learned that. We learned how to survive on our own. Isn't it strange, I sound like I'm the child and you are the mother. But at the same time I feel so old."

"You aren't old."

She smiles and her face really does look young again; she could be the bride. "Yes I am. But that isn't so bad. I think that with all our talk of how Elysia didn't accept the Old Ones, we were all just as afraid of age as anyone there. But somehow when you left and winter came, and then you returned bringing spring, I felt less afraid. Even if you leave again. Paradise is not just timeless gardens. It is rebirth which needs death first."

"Can you still read my thoughts?" I ask her.

"No. Not anymore." There is the slightest breath of sadness or regret in her voice.

She takes my hands and looks into my eyes.

I am afraid of the love I feel. It is so big. I am afraid it will make me want to become a baby again and hide inside of her. But instead I meet her gaze. I feel calm and strong.

"Well," she says, "maybe a little."

"A little what?"

"I can read your thoughts a little." And she kisses my cheek. Both our tears flow, but I know which are mine and which are hers.

With my mother and Zephyra at my side and the women playing drums and flutes behind me, I dance toward the group of men beating their drums beside the waterfall. The veil of water seems as hot as the torches the men bear, for it gives off mist like smoke and glimmers in the fire and moonlight. My own veil is as sheer as water and seems to fall liquid across my face; I can even feel the wet drops on my lashes and my lips. Or is that from tears? The women hold a canopy of flowers floating over our heads like an island, like our desert paradise itself.

The men and women meet on the bank.

My father comes to me. His face is solemn; he is thinner than when I left and the tips of a few curls are turning gray.

"You are so grown up, Primavera."

He does not say it with longing, as if he is wishing for me to be his little girl again, but with pride. Still I know he thinks of the time when I was a child and all his.

I whisper, "I dance Papa I'm dancing I'm dancing up hills evermore I love my heart I can dance I have a flute evermore I love to sing and dance."

His eyes fill with tears and I kiss his rough face. He smells of herb-fires and wine. "Don't cry, Papa. The little dolls are getting wet."

He smiles at me the way he used to when I thought of myself only as a tiny figure in his pupil. But I know that if I looked deep into his eyes now I would not see a child but a grown bride. He takes my hand and leads me to my lover.

Pyre is surrounded by the men. He is one of them and yet he is not like them. I am aware suddenly, perhaps for the first time, of the strange and almost terrifying quality of his beauty. My father releases my hand. I bow my head before Pyre and he kneels on his slender legs. My mother and Zephyra help me climb up on his back. His hair is groomed smooth and slightly damp with mist. His skin has not turned golden like the rest of ours, but a slightly silvered color as if his pallor was dipped in moonlight. Heavy orchids wreathe his chest, the color of sublime wounds. The dancing playing men and women make a circle around us.

Pyre rears onto his hind legs and I cling to him, feeling his back slide between my thighs. Paul gives him an amphora full of wine. He takes both handles and lowers his face into the jar, then twists his neck so that his face is near mine. His lips are as dark and glistening as his eyes. He kisses me, spilling the cool heady liquid into my mouth. The men and women cry out and the music grows louder.

Everyone dances, whirling, waving vine-twined staffs. Where Rafe steps, fountains spring, or is that just an illusion of spilled wine? Fire seems to burst from the tips of Paul's hair, or is that just torchlight? I see him take Rafe in his arms.

Paul's eyes meet mine over Rafe's shoulder, and maybe for the first time I recognize Paul. He is not the god, not the lover, not the father.

Rafe and Paul come toward me. The three of us hold hands and move in a circle. I have never seen Paul like this, free as a child who doesn't care if anyone is watching him or not. I recognize him. He is, finally, my friend.

Life-sized bread sculptures in the shapes of men, women, beasts, creatures, and trees are assembled on the dining island in the middle of the Sound. We eat, tasting the golden crusts, the soft, sweetish, nutty insides, washing it down with wine and water so clear you can taste it glisten. Some people jump into the Sound and eat from the mountains of fresh fruit, edible flowers and herbs piled on lily pads, lit by the floating candles. A cake, all aflame, comes down toward us on its own boat. Made of honey, almond meal, apples, cherries, dates, wine, and mysterious spices the color of powdered jewels, it is as tall as the child who steers the boat. The child is River. The eerie tightness in his face is gone and his head is covered with a wild crown of blue feathers that grow from his scalp. He is no longer a hungry plucked child of Neverland.

I kneel by the shore and take his hand as he steps from the boat.

"Fairy. Thank you for bringing me to your Garden," he whispers.

I put my arms around him, feeling how much stronger he has grown already. The blue feathers are soft against my face.

"Thank *you*, River." I want to tell him that if I hadn't met him I might not have been able to recognize Zephyra as my guide. I might not have been able to recognize my lover with his horse's limbs. When I saw River pulling those feathers out, I glimpsed, for the first time, the mutilating thoughts I had toward myself. Perhaps when I told him not to hurt himself I was speaking to myself. But I had not yet learned to listen to my own words.

If I had, I might never have needed to go to Gunn. But then I would not have found Pyre either.

River kisses my cheek—even the touch of his lips is like feathers. I do not have to say the words aloud—how much he means to me. He knows.

"Fairy," he whispers, "This is the wedding of all of us, isn't it?"

"Yes, River."

He steps onto the shore and runs off to find Zephyra. I watch her envelope her child in the cloak of her radiant wings.

She meets my eyes and smiles, beckoning me with a motion of her head. When I am close enough to hear her throaty whisper, she says, "Once you asked me what it was like to be a mother."

I nod.

"Are you afraid?"

"Yes. But I want Pyre's child."

"I think you will have a girl," she says.

"A colt baby," River adds, and when we all laugh I feel a pleasurable kicking in my still-empty womb like a premonition.

After the feast everyone dances again. I climb up on Pyre's back and he whispers, his voice like embers, "Now, my Primavera, the true wedding."

And we run off into the night as a soft rain begins to fall.

Soon, when the dancing is done and the children are asleep, all the lovers will find their partners and join somewhere in this garden that is our home, just as Pyre and I are joined.

PYRE

We lie under the fruit trees in the long sweet rain, kissing again and again, lips excavating soul-fruit, the nectar of the heart. We spend hours and hours entering, contracting, limbs sealed, healed in heat, the sweat slide sacred ritual. In our lovemaking we live lives. The fetal stage of tender strokes and murmurings, hearing the nourishing heartbeat, sipping the ambrosia milk. Then older child at play, tangle and untangle, hair full of flowers. The youth exploring darkness, those secret places, harsh, fragrant, the coarse, the raw, the torn, the new. And then the mature moment of fulfillment, that racking of the bones with life's convulsions. Here we face all fear, all desire, here we may comfort forth from darkness every demon and bestow with healing breath, transforming the hatred to something exquisite, tremulous. In our quiet aftermath, age old, we settle into silence, touch each other with that tenderness again. Yes, I have seen life, yes, and all here in the circle of our pelvises and all here to the rhythms of our hearts we sleep.

PAUL AND RAFE

His sweat and the rain bathe my face and I feel my flesh settling smooth against the bone, scars dissolving. In this way too, the Sound licks over the pitted earth. Above us on the banks a stone man kneels and drinks his fill from the moonlight that is water. Rafe is these sheer lapping fans of wetness that could be moon or star gloss, could be tears shed by the grateful flowers or our sweat pouring off of us in pale sheets, our fluid pearling the petals white.

Paulo. When he holds me I wonder how I could have gone so long without his touch. His hands blaze as he presses them to my temples. He is the priest of spirit with his harsh cheek and jawbones, but his lips, the heat of his skin, his flame-hair belong to a priest of flesh desire. I kneel at his altar. The white robe falls off his shoulder. His skin is sun-glazed even though it is night and raining. I ride the powerful golden chariot of his body into the blinding light. His gripping jaw releases and song like a sunrise awakens from his throat.

Our bodies struggle on the verge of fury before the surrender. Then our souls surge through and fill the air with rainbows as sun strikes water, water sun.

Rainbows pour back into the earth and the fruit trees rise up like a band of slender young men. In the arms of their branches, they hold guitars and drums, playing a song that comes from the depths of their roots and flares up through their leaves like blood in veins.

We wondered if we could ever have a child but you, Rafe, are my child and I yours as I hold you against my chest my slender son and our child is this love we have made palpable as if a third heart beat between our hard chests. An old man like me—who would have thought it? That many voyages underground and I've resurfaced here now on this wedding day like a youth, smooth and warm, drunk on rainbows, singing to the skies my lover's name.

CALLIOPE AND DIONISIO

We are young again, Dionisio.
I remember the way it felt when you came

and I was sure I had conceived. The egg swelling suddenly, trembling as my body contracted to keep you in me. I shouted out your name. Instead of our velvety bed in that cold sparkling city, I believed we were dancing in some flower forest surrounded by wild beasts and that we were the egg and sperm joining in the earth's womb just as egg and sperm joined in me.

I had forgotten that moment. There had been so much sorrow around us, so much sorrow afterwards. Then when we were all finally safe in the Desert, we grew busy with our child, the mysteries of the land. We still made love, but not like that one time when we still longed for what had not yet bloomed.

Tonight my body remembers.

That night I knelt and brought you down over me. We were balanced like the stones in one of Rafe's sculptures. Then I tipped you backwards against the amethyst satin and slid deeper into you.

You opened your eyes wide, wide and moist, pulling me even deeper until I thought our hipbones would dissolve, our bodies fuse forever, and in your pupils I saw the image of a beautiful young girl. That's when I knew we would have a daughter.

I remember thinking, if we have a child what

will this mean for us? We won't be Elysia children anymore. The responsibility terrified me. I'll really get old now, I thought.

Maybe that is why I couldn't stand to see Primavera so grown up.

But now, tonight, we are young again.

All around us the orchards sing with lovers. The air is like distilled grapes and apple blossoms. And our daughter, who is not a child, has found her lover the way we once found each other and now again, again.

After these long days of not loving, after the dying of the land and the yearning for Primavera, my body, though older—no longer that nymph you roared to as you filled—now I am full of that old joy again. I feel the gardens spilling out from my fingers. You smile as if bathing in wine, my dancing love, eyes and juicy grape curls laughing.

As our daughter and her lover fill the fields with their love, so you and I remember in our willow bed the greening of all things, the beginning of the earth's rebirth.

PRIMAVERA

In the field the flowers grow tall as trees. My love and I lie beneath their canopy. The sun shines through, reflecting lozenges of sheer color onto our naked flesh.

I close my eyes and hear the wind full of pale blue and rose spirits singing our names. I feel the seeds awakening beneath the earth, the water of the Sound running even deeper down. I taste the soothing honey nectar and sharp salt sting of my lover's lips.

I feel my lover's hard large body, so foreign and so known. He is all things. Man and woman, human and beast, strength and softness, joy and sorrow. He is the fire that will burn me pure again, burn away the horror we have seen and leave only gardens.

We live in the orchards of our love. There our child will form in me. The hooves do not make me feel fear. The four small, soft, almost boneless legs tucked under, emerging from me with their hooves. Our child will stand shakily at the edge of this field, looking up at the sky with new eyes. A horse-girl named Arcadie. Spring will come like a wedding, like a festival parade.

I feel as if we are all part of one being—my mother and father, Paul and Rafe, Zephyra and River, Pyre and I. Arcadie, as well. And even Gunn. The Demon is also necessary and inevitable. Once maybe we were all one being, cells made of stars, who split apart or were torn asunder in the wilderness of the universe, created from our destruction, and descended to this world. That is why we all found each other and will continue to join. Forming one song. As River said, my wedding to Pyre is the wedding of all of us.

I may be the voice that sings, but the song is all of ours. And perhaps it will go on and on, scattering flowers in its wake, singing our whole planet back to paradise, joining all the broken pieces together once again.

If you and/or a friend would like to receive the *ROC Advance*, a bimonthly newsletter featuring all the newest and hottest ROC books and authors, on a complimentary basis, please fill out this form and return it to:

ROC Books/Penguin USA
375 Hudson Street
New York, NY 10014

Your Address
Name _____
Street _____ Apt. # _____
City _____ State _____ Zip _____

Friend's Address
Name _____
Street _____ Apt. # _____
City _____ State _____ Zip _____